# We, The Wanted

An Illuminated Gothic Novel

# We, The Wanted

## An Illuminated Gothic Novel

### Matthew Schultz

COSMIC EGG
BOOKS

Winchester, UK
Washington, USA

JOHN HUNT PUBLISHING

First published by Cosmic Egg Books, 2020
Cosmic Egg Books is an imprint of John Hunt Publishing Ltd., 3 East St., Alresford,
Hampshire SO24 9EE, UK
office@jhpbooks.net
www.johnhuntpublishing.com
www.cosmicegg-books.com

For distributor details and how to order please visit the 'Ordering' section on our website.

Text copyright: Matthew Schultz 2019
Illustrations: Jordan Lepore

ISBN: 978 1 78904 325 9
978 1 78904 326 6 (ebook)
Library of Congress Control Number: 2019931228

A CIP catalogue record for this book is available from the British Library.

Design: Stuart Davies

UK: Printed and bound by CPI Group (UK) Ltd, Croydon, CR0 4YY
Printed in North America by CPI GPS partners

We operate a distinctive and ethical publishing philosophy in
all areas of our business, from our global network of authors to
production and worldwide distribution.

# Contents

"What caused us greater concern was the intelligence that met us upon entering the Lake, namely, that the men deputed by our Conductor for the purpose of summoning the Nations to the North Sea, and assigning them a rendezvous, where they were to await our coming, had met their death the previous Winter in a very strange manner. Those poor men (according to the report given us) were seized with an ailment unknown to us, but not very unusual among the people we were seeking. They are afflicted with neither lunacy, hypochondria, nor frenzy; but have a combination of all these species of disease, which affects their imaginations and causes them a more than canine hunger. This makes them so ravenous for human flesh that they pounce upon women, children, and even upon men, like veritable werewolves, and devour them voraciously, without being able to appease or glut their appetite – ever seeking fresh prey, and the more greedily the more they eat. This ailment attacked our deputies; and, as death is the sole remedy among those simple people for checking such acts of murder, they were slain in order to stay the course of their madness."

— *The Jesuit Relations, Volume XLVI, Travels and Explorations of the Jesuit Missionaries in New France 1610–1791.*

For my Dad, old artificer.
M.S.

For Nick, to the moon and back.
J.L.

# Prologue: Fèt Gede

Fausta Delahaye stood at the edge of the woods, her face painted with white chalk to celebrate Fèt Gede, the Haitian Festival of Ancestors. Before her stretched idle train tracks, laid down as a barrier between the town and that cursed wilderness as long ago as the Revolutionary War; behind her, a garish neon glow from the 24-hour gas station cast her shadow toward the treeline. Her dark eyes locked in disbelief on a creature that had emerged from the woods. It stood with one hand still grasping the trunk of an outlying maple. Its fingers disappeared into the bark—as if the thing was an appendage of the tree. It was barely three-feet tall, and with gray skin and long, greasy, black hair that fell around its stout, leathery body. It was unlike anything Fausta had ever seen. The creature's pointed ears hung like those of a jackrabbit, and the twisted horns of a goat grew from its hideous head. The gnarled figure motioned its free hand in a brash coaxing gesture, and repeated a foreign, yet kindly phrase beckoning Fausta to follow: "Ee wahn chu. Kyre."

She squeezed the woman's hand tighter.

"Easy child," a calm voice assured her, "We'll not follow that one into the darkness." The woman's right hand, trembling with age, emerged from the folds of a black, long-sleeved kaftan dress to present Fausta with a photograph of a Vodou priestess dressed in a white, linen shirt and a haint-blue, patchwork dress. She stood upon a patch of dirt before the uneven wood siding of a bayou cabin, wearing a white cap on her head and wingtip tap shoes on her feet. She did not smile, nor did she scowl. Her inscrutable gaze somehow comforted Fausta.

The woman passed Fausta the photograph along with a jar of clear rum infused with red chilies. "Drink."

Fausta did as she was instructed. Tears welled up in her eyes, and when the burn in her throat subsided enough for her to speak, she asked, "What is that thing?"

# Part I

# The Great Hunger

1

# Chapter One

# The Gaeltacht

"Sé do bheatha, a Mhuire—"
Schickt.
"Atá lán de ghrásta—"
Schickt.
"Tá an Tiarna leat."
Schickt.
"Is beannaithe thú idir mná—"
Schickt.
"Agus is beannaithe toradh do bhroinne, Íosa."
Schickt.
"A Naomh-Mhuire, a Mháthair Dé—"
Schickt.
"Guigh orainn na peacaigh—"
Schickt.
"Anois, agus ar uair ár mbáis."

A harsh wind blew over the newly filled graves toward the Cliffs of Moher and across the Atlantic Ocean below, scattering to the sea those final lines of the prayer for the intercession of the Blessed Virgin Mary. A meager group of mourners clutched their rosary beads and closed their tired eyes against the sting of the prayer's final line: "In the hour of our death." Their heads remained bowed in reverence and malnourished exhaustion.

Schickt. An emaciated Patrick Gallagher drove his spade into the moist earth one final time and leaned heavily into it for support. His shirt, yellowed with sweat and dirt, was unbuttoned to his atrophied navel. A pair of worn suspenders had slid from his bony shoulders to hang at his knees; his hair similarly hung about his shoulders, unwashed, unkempt. Patrick's trousers were soiled with the clay from the grave he had been digging, and the added weight threatened to pull them from his waist. Nonetheless, he was handsome. The salt-and-pepper of his beard suited him, and hid his gaunt cheeks. His eyes, the brownish-green of sea froth, focused on the too-fresh mounds of dirt beneath his aching feet.

The service had concluded, and the keening women filed back toward the chapel seeking solace from the cold rain that had begun to anoint the dead in their final resting place. The priest waved his hand over the grave mounds in the sign of the cross. He invited Patrick aside to hand him a small package of seaweed and baked whitefish as payment for his labor. It was a bounty in the gravedigger's lank fingers.

"Thank you," Patrick managed before tearing into the paper and scooping a heap of fish and salted kelp into his mouth. He hadn't eaten in days and chewed with the excitement of someone who had lost all hope of ever again tasting food.

The priest was disgusted, but sympathetic. "There is a ship––" he began.

"A coffin ship," Patrick interjected. A piece of kelp fell from his teeth. Patrick stooped to retrieve it from the mud and shoved it into his mouth along with some ancillary detritus.

The priest, frowning, said nothing. Then, "Nonetheless," he wheezed. The cold air tightened his chest almost to the point of asphyxiation.

"When?" Patrick asked.

"Tomorrow," the priest said. He straightened his hunched shoulders and set rigid his face for he knew what was to come.

Patrick stopped chewing to offer the priest a smile of disappointment. "I suppose the next hole I dig will be for Michael," Patrick spit. Both men knew that—short of committing some grave wrong— there was no hope of scraping together the necessary funds on such short notice.

At this the priest responded, pettish and angry, "There is a way."

* * *

Schickt...

Schickt...

Schickt...

The sun had long wilted below the horizon, and storm clouds shrouded any light the moon or stars may have provided the two men at work among the tombs. The night seemed to condone their sin, having emptied the sky of all witnesses. Patrick, shoulder deep in the ground, used his spade to scrape wet earth away from another burial box, exposing the rusted coffin nails. The priest leaned over the grave to hover his lamp nearer the box so that Patrick could better see his work. In his free hand, the priest clutched a Bible as if to guard himself against this dark deed, which he had proposed.

The nails screamed as Patrick pried them loose, causing the priest to recoil. He scanned the darkness to make sure no one was watching while Patrick removed the lid and drew open the mouth of the corpse. He used two fingers to push aside the rigid tongue and retrieved from beneath it a single florin—payment for Charon to ferry the dead's soul across the river Styx. Patrick turned it over in his hand and rubbed his thumb across the harp opposite Queen Victoria's bust before dropping it into his pocket with the others. "Thank God for superstition," he said to the priest.

"Blasphemy," the priest coughed as Patrick scrambled from the hole, spade in hand, and set to work on the next plot. The priest, despite his hubris, was arrested with fright. He could not tear his gaze from the corpse—its mouth hung open in mute protest—seeming to sneer at him. *Him!*

Schickt...

Schickt...

Schickt...

The sound of Patrick's spade once again carving the ground

compelled the priest to collect himself, and to concentrate on the task at hand. As he moved among the plots, he stole a look back upon the dozens of unearthed caskets, their disrupted inhabitants silently petitioning the empty sky.

The priest vomited on his boots, drawing the attention of Patrick. "For this, there is no absolution," said the priest, wiping bile from his lips. He backed away from Patrick in the direction of the parochial house, shielding himself with his Bible at arm's length. "You did this!"

Patrick set his jaw and said through gritted teeth, "We did this." He drove the spade into the ground and walked out of the cemetery littered with exhumed corpses, laden with shame and the currency of the dead.

Schickt.

\* \* \*

"Wake up," Patrick hissed in the darkness. He shook the blanketed form, "Rory!"

"Huh," Rory asked, sluggish. Pulling the covers back from his face he recognized the anxious eyes of his brother, "What is it, Pat?"

"Gather your things. We're going," Patrick said.

"Where—" Rory began.

"Cork. There's a ship leaving in the morning. We've got to hurry," Patrick explained with haste as Rory rolled out of bed and began pulling on his rags. "There's a mail coach waiting for us at the convent."

"Slow down, Pat! What's going on," Rory asked, trying to understand the urgency. "Are we in trouble?" He ran a hand through his hair and smacked at his face to sharpen his senses.

At this, some of the others in the surrounding beds had stirred awake and were watching the men scramble. Chronic coughing and incessant moaning reverberated off the stone walls, making it sound as if the dying were attempting to commune with the dead. Every bed in the Ennistymon Union Workhouse was occupied, some with as many as five people huddled together on a single mattress. Entire families, evicted from their homes by bankrupt landlords who ushered them into the workhouses as they fled their debts to America, rotted together. Others suffered alone, outcasts with nowhere to turn: unwed mothers, bastards, orphans, lunatics, idiots, and tramps. They would all die in that room from starvation, exhaustion, or disease. How, they all wondered, were these two men escaping their certain doom.

Patrick helped his brother pack the bedding from his bunk into a burlap sack, the only items available to steal. As he surveyed the sores plaguing Rory's hands and face, Patrick wondered if it was cruel to force him on this impossible journey.

"Rory—" he started.

Guessing at Patrick's apprehension, Rory implored him, "Don't leave me here, Pat. Not in this damned place. You can't!"

Patrick gathered his brother into an embrace that he used to help the man to his feet. He shouldered both of their bags and led them out of the sleeping quarters into a long, fetid hallway. "We've got to make a run for it, or the coach might leave without us," he said to Rory, then took off toward the exit. The men fled the workhouse uninhibited. The high walls and iron gates were designed to keep people out of that most hated and feared place in all of Ireland, not in.

The rain had slowed to a drizzle, and the clouds thinned enough for moonbeams to filter through their sinister silhouettes. The convent was only a short distance from the workhouse, and, to Patrick's surprise, the men covered the span quickly. A mail coach that had been arranged by the priest to transport them to Cork met them at the gates.

Patrick waved to the driver, who scowled down at him from his perch above the four horses. Someone inside the cab opened the door for Rory, who was surprised to see a woman and a small boy of about five years of age waiting for them to enter.

"Who are they," Rory asked the coachman.

"Just get in," Patrick said to his brother who was still hesitating on the step. He pushed Rory from behind to speed their boarding. Once settled on the bench across from the woman, Patrick asked, "All set?"

She silently nodded her affirmation and returned her attention to the boy.

"Pat," Rory asked.

"Benefactors," Patrick said, fastening the door. At the click of the latch, the coachman whipped the horses into a gallop.

The road was rocky and rutted, causing the passengers to lurch about the cab. Nonetheless, the boy had fallen asleep in his mother's lap. She stroked his hair and cradled his back to keep him from falling to the floor. They rode in silence for over an hour. The only sounds that breached the cabin were the coachman's bark and the pounding of the horses' hooves, which was so loud that the passengers could not hear the patter of rain upon the roof.

They had passed through Limerick and were headed south beyond Croom Castle when the woman finally fell asleep. Her body slumped forward, enveloping the boy. Patrick continued to stare out the window into the darkness, trying to forget what he'd done to get them there. Rory had not taken his eyes off the child sleeping peacefully in his mother's lap despite the rough ride.

"Is that your boy, Pat," Rory summoned the courage to ask. His tone was simultaneously worrisome and accusatory.

"No," Patrick replied without looking at his brother," "Father Shannon."

"Shite," Rory breathed.

"That boy is the reason we're freed from this place," Patrick said.

"How's that," Rory asked.

"The bishop ordered the priest to send him away," Patrick explained. "I suppose you might think of me as his shepherd."

"So, you knew," Rory said.

"Aye. I inadvertently witnessed the deed," Patrick said.

"Rape," Rory asked.

Patrick did not immediately answer.

"Pat—" Rory started.

"What do you think," Patrick barked, hoping not to recall the image of the priest driving himself into the woman pinned against the cold stone wall in the darkened chapel. Or worse, her plea for help.

"How," is all Rory could summon.

"I was on my way home from the pub. And when I passed St. Joseph's, I saw the oil lamp still burning for Perpetual Adoration. My head was swimming in Tullamore Dew, so I decided to stop for a rest, but found the doors locked. I thought I might just sleep under the archway of the side entrance for a while to allow my mind to clear. It was dark and hidden from the road, so I was sure to be left alone, especially at that hour. But, when I rounded the corner, I found the door unlatched, so I stepped inside for the warmth of the place. I didn't have both feet across the threshold before I spied them across the nave. The host was still in the monstrance…"

"Jaysus," Rory swore.

"…The priest must have heard the door creak or felt the cold rush in. He turned his head immediately to look at me from over his shoulder. He had her pushed against the wall, her face thrust in the corner. She must have sensed my presence as well because I heard her sob a single word: 'Please.' I was too dazed to move forward. The priest's face peeled into an awful smirk and he continued his business with her. Horrified and ashamed, I fled."

Rory looked at the woman sitting across from him with pity. "Does she know it was you could have stopped it?"

Patrick shook his head, his gaze intent upon the darkness

beyond the coach. "It's not the worst that man has done, either," Patrick ended his tale, "to her, or to me."

"Then why the bloody hell are you helping him?" Rory demanded with disbelief—unsure what could be worse than what he's just heard, and unwilling to speculate.

"I didn't volunteer," Patrick lamented, finally turning to face Rory. "It was this or the Judas Cradle."

* * *

When they arrived at the dockyard the sun still slumbered in twilight, but the dim embers of dawn had transformed the River Lee into a ruptured vein emptying its crimson flush into the Celtic Sea. The black silhouettes of ships' masts and standing rigging looked to the forlorn travelers like bodies impaled upon war pikes; the dense row of passengers lining the waterfront in preparation for boarding became another funeral procession.

"Wait here," Patrick said and disappeared into the crowd. He was heading toward the dock attendant stationed next to the boarding ramp barred by crates of various sizes.

Rory slumped to the ground among the scores of other famished bodies. "I'm Rory, by the way. Pat's brother," he said and offered the woman standing next to him with her son in her arms a sympathetic smile.

"Kate," she replied, "and this is Michael." The boy didn't stir. He had spied an apple cart not too far off and watched as men in suits exchanged coins for fruit. He knew better than to ask his mother if he might have one.

"Have you got any relations in America," Rory asked.

"No," Kate responded. "We haven't got any here, either."

"Aye," Rory said. "We've got an uncle up in Highbridge. He left Ireland in '37 to work on the Croton Aqueduct. Pat and I have been planning to join him for some time, but haven't been able to gather the means to make the crossing."

"I know," Kate said.

"Oh, yeah," Rory said, realizing that she and Patrick had been slaves to Father Shannon for years. "So, you're coming with us, then?"

"I suppose. At least at first. We've haven't got another option," Kate admitted.

"Are you and Pat—" Rory began to pry.

"No," Kate declared.

"Of course, sorry," Rory said.

"I couldn't," Kate explained, "with anyone."

"Mama! Look!" Michael exclaimed. Kate turned around to see Patrick approaching with apples in his hands and papers clenched in his teeth.

He first tossed an apple to Rory, then handed one to Michael and Kate who graciously accepted. They each savored their fruit, and when only cores remained, Patrick revealed a parcel of salted pork. He unwrapped the meat and handed the first piece to Michael who clapped his hand with glee.

"Thank you, Pat! Mama, look!" Michael said, smiling. He held the flesh to his nose and breathed deep before taking a bite.

"Yes, thank you," Kate said to Patrick and kissed his cheek. She looked at Michael through tears that welled up in her eyes.

"It's so yummy!" Michael said.

Kate squeezed him and said to the brothers, "I don't think he's ever been so happy."

"Any luck with the tickets," Rory interjected, hopeful.

"Full up," Patrick reported. "But, I was able to purchase three from a family that was willing to part with them for twice their cost."

"Three," Rory said, dejected.

"Aye, three tickets for the *Agnes*," Patrick said.

Kate frowned at Rory, whose escape had been cut off.

"And one for passage on the *Marion*," Patrick added with a devilish grin.

"You arse!" Rory exclaimed, jumping up to embrace his brother.

"The ships leave port together," Patrick said as the line of passengers began shuffling toward the boarding ramps. He gave Rory his papers for the *Marion*. "We'll be quarantined at La Gross Île just outside Quebec City, where we can catch a steamer down the Hudson."

"A steamship!" Kate gasped.

"Well then, I'll see you all in Canada!" Rory said and hugged Patrick farewell. Rory waved to Kate and tussled Michael's hair as he skipped past them to the far dock.

"Stay above deck as often as you can. You'll have less chance of catching the fever should it break out," Patrick yelled.

"May the wind be ever at our backs," Rory called back triumphantly. "I can't wait to see the look on Uncle Pete's face when the Gallagher brothers finally show up in Highbridge!"

## Chapter Two

# Black Atlantic

## ADVICE
## TO
## IRISH EMIGRANTS

IN the UNITED STATES, labour is there the *first* condition of life, and industry is the lot of all men. Wealth is not idolized; but there is no degradation connected with labour; on the contrary, it is *honorable*, and held in general estimation.

In the remote parts of America, *an industrious youth* may follow any occupation without being looked down upon or sustain loss of character, and he may rationally expect to *raise himself* in the world by his labor.

In America, *a man's success* must altogether rest with himself – it will depend on his *industry, sobriety, diligence* and *virtue*; and if he do not succeed, in nine cases out of ten, the cause of failure is to be found in the *deficiencies* of his own character.[1]

"It's quite small," Kate observed nervously. "Do you think we'll make it alright?"

"I think its size is the least of our worries," Patrick said. He had finished reading a flyposting lacquered to the spar with wheat paste and began eyeing a man who was clutching at his stomach and sweating despite the crisp morning air.

"I suppose," Kate said, following Patrick's stare.

"I saw the crew loading crates of whale oil earlier. One hogshead of that stuff is more valuable than the lot of us. They wouldn't load it onto a ship at risk of ending up on the bottom of the ocean," Patrick reassured her.

"I suppose," Kate repeated.

Suddenly a voice boomed, "Anchors aweigh," and the ship

eased away from the dock. Michael wriggled his hand from his mother's grasp to squeeze through the crowded deck toward the ship's railing, where he could wave to no one in particular on the docks. He was happy. The smell of salt water on the calm breeze carried with it the promise of adventure the likes of which he had never experienced. Tales of merrymaking pirates, deserted islands, and trunks of gold washed before him: The sorts of pirate tales innocence-preserving nuns told to rambunctious little boys. Michael watched seagulls glide among the ship's tall masts. Every now and again they would dip into the waves and emerge with breakfast. He envied them, even if he didn't yet have such words to describe how he felt.

As the boat sailed slowly down the river toward the sea, passengers had begun to file below deck to claim their bunks. Most of them would remain in their holds for the duration of the voyage for fear of losing their coveted space. At the cabin doors, a midshipman handed each adult three days' rations of sea biscuits, which many of them consumed almost immediately despite the stomach-wrenching stench emanating from below. From sunup to sundown, the cabins were ovens intensifying that foul odor that did not discriminate between bankrupt Lords and devastated peasants. None of the hundreds of fleeing refugees were immune to the reek of rotten food, rotten flesh, shit, tobacco smoke, vomit, stale perspiration, and mildewed clothes. It was near impossible to breathe, which is why a good many elected to remain above deck while others crawled ever deeper into the bowels of the ship to camp among the bundles and chests of the steerage quarters. Patrick, Kate, and Michael elected to journey in the open air. They did not, however, suffer any less given the scorch of the sun nor the frigid night air.

A midshipman announced that their journey to port would take between six weeks and three months, depending on the weather. Patrick's thoughts were elsewhere. He was more concerned that he hadn't yet seen the *Marion* emerge from the

River Lee, and when he asked about it, none of the crew could offer him any information. One deckhand assumed that they got held up waitin' for, "a bunch of worthless bog-trotters to board."

"Would they do that," Patrick pressed. "Would they delay the launch to wait for additional passengers?"

"At five pounds per head the captain would be damned to leave anyone behind," the deckhand said. And, just as the *Agnes* was rounding Robert's Head, Patrick spied the delayed ship following in their distant wake. Relieved, he squeezed in along the railing next to Michael and Kate to watch as the water sped by below them. Patrick had wondered at the reason he so easily procured a spot aboard the *Marion* for his brother. He recalled stories told of ships being bought cheaply from salvage yards and put into transatlantic rotation with little to no maintenance. But Patrick hadn't seen any signs of black rot nor neglect, and the sails looked to be hardly weathered. It now seemed likely the captain had seized an opportunity to line his own pockets by cutting the ship's owner out of the transaction. A ticket out of Ireland is a ticket out of Ireland, Patrick thought, justifying to himself the means of paying for their passage with the promise of a new beginning in America.

Somewhere a balladeer played shanties on a fiddle that would not hold its tuning. A few measures into each song the instrument became raucous, setting the other passengers on edge. Worse still, no one could locate the bard to put an end to the jarring noise that seemed to echo from every open hatch. The music continued long after the Blasket Islands had disappeared beyond the horizon leaving only open water stretching as far as the eye could see in any given direction. Many of the passengers tempered the grate of the music with long swigs from the bottles of rotgut whiskey dancing from hand to hand.

By the end of the first day, an air of relief and mild excitement—aided by some drunken merriment—had taken hold of the *Agnes*. Patrick admitted an apprehension to Kate concerning the *Marion*, which he hadn't seen since it entered into the Celtic Sea earlier that morning. But a Dubliner sitting nearby who had overheard Patrick's worry assured him, "I've worked a number of fishing boats off Howth Head for the past 15 or so years, and each one would cut the water a bit differently."

"Oh?" Patrick asked.

"Factor in the unequal passenger and cargo weights and it's not unlikely that a boat only a few knots slower than another would be lost to the naked eye for the duration of an ocean crossing."

"I guess that seems possible," Patrick accepted.

"I'm sure Rory is fine, Pat," Kate assured him.

"Maybe I can borrow a spyglass to see a bit further," Patrick said.

"A spyglass doesn't allow you to see farther," the fisherman corrected him. "It only makes those things that are already in view bigger. You'll have to resign yourself to the fact that we are all at the mercy of the trade winds—or go mad staring at the horizon for a month. And go mad you will."

"I know," Patrick said, though it was unclear if he agreed with the fisherman about the spyglass, the trade winds, or his impending madness.

\* \* \*

The *Agnes* had been at sea for nearly five weeks without incident. Good fortune meant that only twelve passengers had thus far died due to fever and dysentery. Each had been laid to rest in the depths of the Atlantic with appropriate ceremony:

| | | |
|---|---|---|
| James Aylard, 18 | John Barry, 30 | Patrick Barry, 50 |
| Mary Coakley, 18 | Thomas Coakley, 24 | Thomas Crane, 11 months |
| John Cronin, 10 | Timothy Deenan, 36 | Hodly Finn, 3 |
| Andrew Neill 25 | Mary Murphy, 18 months | Judith Sullivan, 22[2] |

At that time, another 29 souls were quarantined below deck. That number was sure to wax and wane as more passengers contracted the looming death. The hatches had been locked to help contain a widespread outbreak, but no healthy passenger was willing to enter the hold to care for the sick. Human waste sloshed back and forth across the floor with every pitch of the bow, soaking the sick in their own excrement. Lice and flies ate at their burning flesh. The dying could hear the heavy clomping of feet above that caused the floorboards to creak with exhilaration. They each fantasized in their own way about breaking the hatch locks to join their loved ones in the fresh ocean air—either for a comforting embrace or to throw themselves overboard to end their torment.

Meanwhile, Captain Thomas McCawley listened with sympathy to the moans emanating from below his feet while he toured the deck, smoking his evening pipe. Ultimately, he had been responsible for bolting the sick inside the quarantine cabin, condemning them not only to certain but also vile death. He therefore never looked directly at any of the other passengers— the friends and relatives of those damned below—but instead scanned the mass of them as one.

His weathered lips sipped at the vulcanite stem of his favorite Billiard-shaped pipe, carefully ripening the ash into a smoldering cherry before drawing a deeper breath. He held it for a moment, savoring his evening treat. Then he released a plume of milky Latakia smoke past his yellowed mustaches and into the air. The cloud drifted past a lone passenger leaning against the starboard railing; his head hung low beneath his slumped shoulders. The smell of peat fire was something of a small comfort to the homesick Irishman.

Patrick Gallagher turned to face the captain, who pulled a brass cigarette case from the inside pocket of his navy-blue P-jacket and offered it to him. Patrick accepted. "My brother used to smoke a tobacco that smelled like that," he said.

"Good man!" McCawley roared, extending his hand for Patrick to shake, which he did. "Where's that bother of yours now?"

"On his way to New York," Patrick said. "We'll meet up with him in Quebec City once we're released from quarantine."

"Oh?" McCawley asked. He struck a match and cupped his hands around the flame. He held it for a moment to make sure it took to the timber. Patrick leaned in to light his cigarette. Once lit, McCawley watched the flame die between his fingers. "Ah, even that little bit of heat feels good upon the old joints."

Patrick nodded in agreement; his own hands shoved into his pants pockets to hide them from the cold. "How about the *Agnes*, where's she headed after Quebec?" Patrick attempted to make conversation as a way of thanking the captain for the smoke.

"Back to Cork," McCawley said, happy for the chat. "I live in this puddle between two banks of the same hell."

"So, you're the ferryman," Patrick said.

"Charon? Aye, that's me," McCawley agreed with a wink. "You believe in monsters, then?"

Patrick grasped the few remaining coins nested in the depths of his pockets. Then let them fall away to pluck the cigarette from his lips, "I do."

"Good," the captain said cheerfully. "It might just keep you alive." He poked Patrick in the chest with the oxidized stem of his pipe.

"Death is not the worst punishment," Patrick said.

"No," the captain agreed, and his tone darkened. "It is not."

Patrick was startled by this change and looked for a way to end their conversation, "I was led to believe there would be no questions."

The captain pulled a fleck of tobacco from his tongue, "I like to know who's on my ship. I'm especially curious about how the likes of you can afford the passage. Evicted, I'd bet? Were you lucky enough to have one of the God-fearing landlords willing to pay your way to America?"

"I knew a priest with a secret," Patrick admitted, afraid to be accused of stealing a ticket. Or, worse, of being a stowaway.

"And your priest paid to relocate you," McCawley pressed.

"Something like that. I just hope New York holds more for me than Ireland. It's a big enough city. I suppose I'll make my way," Patrick predicted.

"Lad, if we don't die in quarantine, you're going to have one hell of a hike." Rain had begun to fall on the men.

"I have a few pounds left. That should be enough to catch a ferry in Montreal. My uncle wrote to us of steamboats plying the Hudson between the St. Lawrence and Manhattan," Patrick explained. "He's working as a hod carrier in the Bronx—"

At this McCawley howled. "No Irishman can afford a ride on a steamboat! And if you can, you'll be arrested for larceny!" A thunderclap cut short McCawley's laughter. He scrunched up his face to study the sky before turning back to Patrick with an unsettled look in his eye, "You had better get below deck. That's an angry sky if ever I've seen one. Our luck may have just run out." Without another word, the captain hustled back to the quarterdeck. The storm arrived, and the waters churned.

Patrick flicked his unfinished cigarette into the ocean below, twisting and writhing like an undulating serpent. The orange streak of lighted ash dove toward the angry waves like a cannon shot until it disappeared in an instant. Passengers were hurrying in all sorts of directions in search of cover or mooring. Some had preemptively slipped into lifeboats; others had risked the feverish hell below deck. Patrick didn't know what to do, so he joined a group of about twenty men, women, and children huddled around the main mast. A rope ran around the circumference of the group securing them together despite the ship's violent pitch from side to side. He managed to squirm into the bunch before the first of the waves burst over the ship.

A hand reached out through the mass of bodies to grasp

Patrick's shoulder. He followed the length of the appendage back to its owner and saw Kate's horrified expression.

"We'll be alright," he yelled. "Where's Michael?" Kate couldn't hear him over the deafening sound of the waves battering the small vessel.

She was, however, able to read his lips, and motioned down and in front of her. He must be tied directly to the mast at the center of the scrum, Patrick thought. As he searched for Michael's curly hair in the crowd, the ship rolled within a few degrees of capsizing. Screams rang out louder than the storm itself.

Patrick alone experienced a moment of serenity. As quickly as the *Agnes* had been pushed into a horizontal position parallel to the waters below, it was once again standing upright, lifted high by a second monstrous wave. And from atop that watery mountain, Patrick spied the dim glow of another ship's navigation light in the southern distance.

"*Marion*," Patrick breathed with relief, and sea swell filled his mouth. He choked it out onto the back of the man in front of him and was able to fill his lungs with air before the *Agnes* slid down the wave's rushing slope into a perilous valley below. Another crest broke over her deck. All of the sailors who hadn't secured themselves to the ship were washed overboard alongside the bodies of the previous day's dead, already wrapped in sailcloth for a morning burial at sea. That single wave had doubled the death toll aboard the *Agnes*.

* * *

Michael's small, lifeless body hung limply against the center mast. The curly hair that Patrick had been looking for amidst the chaos of the storm had been flattened by the deluge. Michael's arms, secured to the timber by shipping rope, appeared to hug the smooth wood while his left cheek pressed heavily into the mast as it would the crook of his mother's neck if he were to fall asleep in her arms. No one could see his pale face.

His mother's bloodied fingers worked frantically at the knots she had tied thrice over to ensure his safety prior to the storm. The saltwater and the pitch of Michel's body weight thrown about by the lurching ship had tightened the knots beyond Kate's strength.

A woman who had hidden a filet knife in her shawl for protection, should she need it, sawed at the thick rope while others who had just crawled from beneath the piles of debris and bloated corpses watched helplessly.

"Tobacco!" Patrick called, and a nearby sailor pulled soggy cigarettes and damp matches from his pants pocket.

"Wet!" he yelled.

"Get the captain," Patrick ordered.

The sawing woman managed to cleave through the ropes, and Kate peeled Michael's body from the mast. She laid him down just as she had on so many banal occasions to tuck him into bed for the night. Kate cradled her boy's face in her lap and wept while Patrick began pressing on his abdomen.

When the sailor arrived with McCawley, he immediately crouched down to lift Michael's legs into the air. McCawley drew smoke through his pipe and blew it forcefully into the boy's mouth.

"What are you doing?" Kate screamed.

"Irritating his lungs," Patrick explained, "to expel the water."

Sorrow filled the silence as the crowd watched the Captain offer a second bellow of smoke to no avail. No one moved. No one breathed. They all waited together aboard the small ship drifting slowly westward on the not-yet-placid waters of the Atlantic. "I'm sorry Miss," McCawley said to Kate. Patrick stopped the compressions to wipe tears from his eyes. "The boy's gone."

The captain moved to close Michael's eyes. "Don't touch him!" Kate growled. McCawley nodded his concession. He clasped Patrick on the shoulder and offered him a sympathetic grimace.

The sawing woman pressed Kate's hand with her own. "He's a lucky one Mum; didn't suffer too greatly. My Johnathan was sick with the fever for weeks before he finally succumbed. They wouldn't even let me below to care for him."

Kate said nothing. She held her baby boy as close to her as she could as if to give him some of her warmth—even in death.

"We was to bury Johnathan tomorrow," the woman continued, "but his body washed overboard in the storm…" Kate couldn't bring herself to look at the woman. She kept her head bent close to Michael's body. Her eyes squeezed shut against the pain. Seeing that her story offered Kate no comfort, the woman trailed off and retreated into the crowd. Patrick attempted to thank the woman for her help, but she had already disappeared into the torture chamber of her own mourning.

Patrick thought of things to say to Kate but settled into a weary silence. He stole a look at Michael's face. It was serene. Gone was the excitement of their journey, but gone, too, was the suffering of famine and illegitimacy. "Death is not the worst punishment." He had said that to McCawley no more than a few hours earlier when thinking only of himself. He was no longer so sure that sentiment was true. Patrick placed a hand upon Kate's cheek to let her know that she was not alone. He instantly felt the fire of her fever. Still, he could say nothing.

Michael was not the only one to die in the storm. Other families were huddled around the corpses of loved ones, saying goodbyes and promising relief in the afterlife. Some of the dead did not have anyone to tend to them, and they lay scattered on the deck waiting for the crew to haul them away. Patrick stepped over these derelict bodies to resume his post at the ship's railing. He squinted his eyes to bring the horizon into focus. The navigation light he had noticed during the storm was nowhere to be found. The *Marion* was nowhere to be found. He wondered if he had imagined it—if madness had begun its insidious embrace.

\* \* \*

It had been three days since the storm—three days of profound grieving for those who had lost their lives within a week of the quarantine station at Gross Île. Eight bodies were arranged on the deck to be washed. Four had prematurely entered their watery graves when they were swept overboard by the same wave that had choked the life out of Michael. Each corpse was covered in white sailcloth and adorned with black ribbons made from one of McCawley's suits. The captain had also filled a range of pipes and offered them to the gathered men. The smoke, he explained, would deter evil spirits from finding the dead. Patrick scoffed at the superstition but smoked nonetheless.

Three nights had passed during which wives and mothers and sisters sat watch over the deceased. They keened, lamenting the loss of their beloved and of those who had no one left to mourn them. The women's cries swelled into wails as passengers lined the deck to pay their final respects. Amidst all this, Kate remained silent.

As Captain McCawley moved toward the railing to begin the funeral rites, Patrick unclasped his hands from behind his back and rested them on Kate's shoulders. She was seated in front of him, her own trembling hands folded in her lap. She hadn't risen from that chair since the fever struck her, but the time had come for Kate to give unto the sea what it had claimed from her already. She half turned to allow Patrick to help her to her feet. Using her remaining strength, she bent down to kiss the shrouded forehead of her only child.

Kate planted a hand on the deck to steady herself as her face hovered above Michael's body. "I loved you from the moment you were conceived," she whispered to him, "despite it all." Without looking up at Patrick, she motioned to him to help her back into the chair. Kate's emotional and physical pain were scorched into her body. She leaned, listless, into Patrick's hip, her arms across her stomach in an attempt to dull the pain. He lowered her into the chair with a frown.

Patrick then hoisted Michael's body up onto his shoulder, leaned over the ship's railing, and lowered it into the sea. He felt instantly unmoored. With his empty hands, Patrick grasped the railing to steady himself. He missed his spade, its worn handle familiar against his rough palms. The feeling of it slicing through the Irish clay. Still, he thought, this is better. Michael will be undisturbed in his slumber beneath the waves—safe from the greedy clutch of grave robbers and resurrectionists. He watched the body sink for as long as it remained visible—a few seconds at most. It seemed to Patrick that life was governed by a handful of moments no longer than the time it took for the boy's ghostly shroud to disappear into the murk. It was the same flash of time in which he locked eyes upon the *Marion* before she, too, vanished between the waves.

"I'm not going to make it to New York," Kate said. Her prediction interrupted Patrick's thoughts.

"No." Patrick agreed without turning to her.

"Promise me that when I die, you'll bring my body back to this spot so that I can be with Michael," Kate said.

"Okay, Kate," Patrick promised, unwilling to pretend that there was any hope for her.

"I said promise," Kate seethed. At this, Patrick turned around. The tone that Kate had conjured forth did not match her failing health.

Resentment flared in her eyes and twisted her mouth into a scowl Patrick had not thought possible. "I promise," he said, unsettled by the wicked look of the dying woman before him.

"You had better, Patrick Gallagher. Or curse you for doing nothing five years ago while that monster raped me in God's house, and curse you for doing nothing now to save my baby boy!"

* * *

On June 10, 1847, the *Agnes* had dropped anchor outside the quarantine station at Gross Île adding to a line of ships already stretched long, like late afternoon shadows down the St. Lawrence River. Each morning over the course of the previous two weeks Patrick would wake up to a thick fog concealing everything from his view that was more than an arm's length away. A purgatory of sorts in which he could see no evil—or, at least, in which he couldn't be seen as evil.

Not until the midday sun had burnt away the cold morning fog could Patrick look east to take stock of the newly moored ships that had arrived in the night. He hadn't set eyes upon the *Marion* since the night of the storm, but neither could he see all of the dozens of vessels detained in the narrow channel outside Québec City. He held out hope that his brother was similarly interned upon a wooden jail floating upon the interstitial waters between the two Canadian provinces of New Brunswick and Québec. Patrick, therefore, spent the early hours of each day in the dark, cavernous holds below the decks scavenging. It wasn't the fog alone, but the anguished cries of the dying reverberating up and down the river that drove Patrick into the ship's invariant blackness.

There was no light in the bowels of the *Agnes* except for the single, flickering flame that Patrick carried with him. The candle was more of a comfort piece than a functional tool as it did little to illuminate his path. Since there were no portholes to brighten the hold, Patrick's circumambulating was never betrayed. He was always careful to close the hatchways behind him for privacy. The consequence was that he cut off any ventilation that might offer some respite from the stench of thirty-five rotting corpses.

The rows of bodies reminded Patrick of the graveyard he had helped plant in the Irish countryside over the past two years. And like his time spent moving dirt in that overpopulated plot of land adjacent to St. Joseph's Chapel, he was not below deck to pay his respects. Patrick moved quickly amongst the dead. He was agile, focusing his efforts upon the middle and upper-class passengers: lords and ladies, MPs, accountants, lawyers, and landlords—villains of the famine. From them, he took buttons, cufflinks, jewelry, even dental crowns. Patrick did not enjoy this work, nor was he excited by the spoils. But he needed currency to buy supplies and to secure transportation for him and his brother to get to New York. The dead had no further expenses on their final pilgrimage, which was to end in the anonymity of a mass grave in the Grosse-Île Eastern Cemetery.

When he finished his work, Patrick escaped the hold as carefully as he had entered it. He slipped past the rows of dead peasants (who he knew had nothing to offer him) as if they weren't even there. Though he did steal a hurried glance at Kate's bloated corpse before exiting the hatchway. Whether out of guilt or affection he couldn't be sure. An exposed foot protruded from beneath the unfastened cloth serving as her burial shroud. A starving rat chewed upon it unabashedly. Patrick threw the remains of his candle at the rat, which scurried from its feast into a nearby hole in the wooden hull. Satisfied with his act of apology and farewell, he emerged into the sunlight and filled his lungs with several deep breaths of clean air before checking himself for louse. The captain leaned against a mast, watching Patrick examine his clothes for parasites.

McCawley called to him, "Poor Orpheus! The gods have wrest your Eurydice's shadow back into the underworld and damned her among the dead."

"Huh?" Patrick jumped. He had thought he was alone. The smell of rot still hanging in his nose masked the aroma of the captain's pipe and his eyes had not yet adjusted to the brightness of midday. "Oh, captain! Erm, just paying my respects before we dock," Patrick said.

"Aye," McCawley said, eyeing the thief.

"I'm glad you're here," Patrick said, "I've got a favor to ask."

"Humpf," McCawley breathed.

"I promised Kate that I'd see to it that she be buried at sea—near her boy," Patrick said.

"Aye," McCawley repeated.

"But I can't make the return trip. I've got to find my brother," Patrick explained.

"And you want me to transport that disease-ridden carcass for free, I presume," McCawley asked.

"I can pay—" Patrick began.

"You'll pay!" McCawley growled. "Full fare."

Patrick assented without argument, which dramatically improved the captain's mood—especially as he had no intent of honoring the agreement. She'd be dumped with the rest of the lot before the ship sailed into the Port of Montreal to deliver their cargo of whale oil.

As Patrick doled out the remaining silver from his pockets, he asked if McCawley had received any word of the *Marion* entering quarantine. Only half of the nearly forty ships rumored to be held in the St. Lawrence were visible from the deck of the *Agnes*, and Patrick was anxious to hear news of his brother's arrival.

"*Marion*? That's a convict transport headed for Port Arthur, Tasmania," McCawley said.

"No," Patrick said. Clearly, the captain had confused the *Marion* with another vessel. "My brother is on that ship. I bought his ticket just before we set sail from Cork."

"Feck." McCawley sighed.

"That can't be. Why would they take Rory on board, then?" Patrick cried.

"Silver," McCawley said. "It's all a profits game. You sold your brother into hard labor."

"That can't be possible! They can't do that! They can't hold an innocent man! We have to contact the authorities!" Patrick yelled.

"The British authorities? They won't give a kangaroo's shite about your peat-farming brother," McCawley said.

"He'll tell them there's been a mistake," Patrick said. "That he's no convict."

"They'll beat him until he can't talk no more. Then they'll lock him in the asylum," McCawley said.

Patrick's disbelief devolved into guilt. He sobbed. "I saw a light in the storm. Another ship. It was the *Marion*." He said the words as if they were fact, hoping his certainty would make them true.

McCawley was contrite, "You did see a ship, lad. A slaver. Lagos to Boston most likely. It's the northernmost route of the Middle Passage, but it wouldn't be uncommon."

"He's already anemic from starvation—" Patrick went silent.

"The fate of the folks on that slaver is no better than what your brother has before him. The New World is a nasty place, and so is the bush. Only the lifers get sent to that island. Maybe there'd be a sliver of hope if he were headed to Botany Bay. Then he'd only be looking at seven or so years of hard labor. But the abuses he'll face…it's not likely he'll last seven weeks if it's true he's in the state you describe."

Patrick slumped to the ground as if to retreat from what the captain had told him. McCawley sidled up next to him in an attempt to pass him something. At first, Patrick didn't look up, but McCawley nudged him with the object to get his attention. "The boy was holding it when he passed."

Patrick raised his eyes to see a worn, leather-bound book. He instantly recognized it as the priest's Bible. He must have gifted it to Michael before sending him away. "You should have left it with him," Patrick said, still thinking of Rory.

"I figured his mother would have wanted it as a keepsake… of course," the captain trailed off as he realized that Patrick had now lost all of his traveling companions.

"I doubt that book would have brought her any comfort,"

Patrick said. "It belonged to the boy's father."

"I see," McCawley said, unsure if he did. "Well, maybe it will bring you a bit of solace." He extended the book again.

Patrick refused it. "God can't protect any of us, Captain."

Defeated, McCawley lowered the book and his eyes.

"Or won't," Patrick concluded.

# Chapter Three

# Wilderness

The sweet, loamy petrichor of the forest had settled Patrick Gallagher's troubled mind. As he slipped among the trees—white pines and eastern hemlocks; black oaks and shagbark hickories—he sang a faery song that transported him back to the familiar Irish woods and Arcadian splendor of his childhood.

> Where dips the rocky highland
> Of Sleuth Wood in the lake,
> There lies a leafy island
> Where flapping herons wake
> The drowsy water rats;
> There we've hid our faery vats,
> Full of berries
> And of reddest stolen cherries.
> *Come away, O human child!*
> *To the waters and the wild*
> *With a faery, hand in hand,*
> *For the world's more full of weeping than you can understand.*[3]

The constant trill of whistling insects was punctuated by the crass calls of circling ravens. Their deep, croaking *kraa–gronk* echoed against the graphite outcroppings that score the High Adirondacks, making it impossible for Patrick to tell how many of the birds were out there and how far away they might be. So much was hidden by the dense growth of the immense forest. Unlike the woodlands he used to roam near his family's cottage in Ballynacally, no paths had been trodden, no trails marked. To guide his steps along the treacherous terrain, Patrick had fashioned a walking stick from a dead tree limb by snapping it across his shinbone to a manageable length. He used the stick to part long grass and to poke at the questionable ground on his way down a steep hill. At the foot of the hill, he noticed a misshapen tree. It may not have appeared to him except that he had noted a similarly unnatural tree a few hours earlier. It was then that he recalled the final words Captain McCawley had spoken to him aboard the *Agnes*: "Follow the trees."

That particular tree, peculiar as it was, was not very large. Patrick guessed that he could wrap his arms around the tree's trunk and still be able to interlace his fingers on the opposite side without much difficulty. What had initially drawn his attention, however, was that its trunk bent at a 90-degree angle only a few feet from the ground. Its back was lacerated, coaxing the main trunk to extended parallel to the ground for five or six feet before shooting straight up into the air. At this second bend toward the sky, a 'nose' protruded as if sniffing out something important in the direction in which it pointed. Upon closer inspection, Patrick noticed scarring at the crook of the second bend as well as a deep fissure around the entire circumference of the 'nose' as if the tree had grown around a shaping rope. He decided to change course toward the direction in which the tree pointed. For, as McCawley had advised him, "Follow the trees. The Injuns bend them to mark the trail. Can't be moved like stones, and can't be erased like a drawing. Those pointed trees should lead you through the rough country, usually toward water or game trails."

And it wasn't long before Patrick came upon another unnaturally bent tree, and then another. Once he began actively looking for them—and following their path—the marker trees appeared at regular intervals about every hundred yards. The trees led him back up the ridge, across the spine of a mountain that dropped into gorged hollows on either side. Patrick followed a leisurely descent that delivered him into a small clearing poxed by vernal pools. Caddis flies flitted among the reeds, and yellow-spotted salamanders slid betwixt tree branches that had collapsed into the water. A pair of wood ducks skimmed the surface of the largest pond, indifferent to Patrick's presence. The water was a muddied brown color and replete with old fallen leaves, reminding Patrick of oatmeal.

The route between ponds was cluttered by downed pines blanketed with thick moss and overgrown Blackberry thorns. Patrick quickly set to foraging, enjoying the tart blackberry juice that quenched his thirst. As he waded deeper into the brush, bright red mushrooms littered the forest floor. The large toadstool caps were spotted with white warts, resembling the fare his mother used to bake and stuff with sage flavored sausage for special occasions. Patrick plucked one from its stem and hazarded a bite. Its flavor was palatable: an earthy, warm spice. Though the raw, rubbery caps were difficult to chew, he ate three of them and picked a handful of others to roast for dinner. With his burlap sack weighted with berries and mushrooms, he set off toward the tree line at the opposite end of the clearing whence he entered, which is when he noticed a series of small stone mounds ringing the far side of the pond.

Each pile of fist-sized rocks looked to be no more than 18 inches high. They had clearly been stacked by someone, and Patrick wondered if these were the stone markers McCawley had mentioned as he disembarked from the *Agnes* weeks earlier. The rock piles didn't appear to point in any direction but rather were simply scattered along the banks of the ponds making it unlikely that they were Indian markers. Patrick cautiously nudged one of the piles over with the toe of his boot. The stones scattered in the long grass but revealed nothing. Bemused, he continued along the bank and into the woods, kicking at the stone piles as he went in hopes that something useful might appear.

The golden glow of watchful eyes leered at Patrick from the dense underbrush. As he entered back into the shadowy forest, a silent horde of goblin-like creatures slunk after him—their dark bodies all but invisible. A few of the stout creatures remained behind to reconstruct the stone mounds Patrick had kicked over before rejoining the others in his wake. They worked quickly to stack the stones despite their clawed fingers and cloven feet. Patrick, unaware that he was being followed by the incensed púca, continued his song:

> Where the wave of moonlight glosses
> The dim gray sands with light,
> Far off by furthest Rosses
> We foot it all the night,
> Weaving olden dances
> Mingling hands and mingling glances
> Till the moon has taken flight;
> To and fro we leap
> And chase the frothy bubbles,
> While the world is full of troubles
> And anxious in its sleep.
> *Come away, O human child!*
> *To the waters and the wild*
> *With a faery, hand in hand,*
> *For the world's more full of weeping than you can understand.*

Moonbeams filtered through the leafy canopy, glittering upon the forest floor. In the darkness, the trees seemed to rise toward the spectral light of the moon. Patrick thought that he could hear the trees growing. They groaned like a root torn from dirt, or a vine ripped from the bark of its host. He told himself that he was getting tired and that the distortions were simply shadows preying on his exhausted mind. He'd find a safe place to bed down for the night and get an early start in the morning.

But then he began to feel dizzy as the forest moved around him. It was one thing when the trees looked to be sprouting upwards into the night sky, but it was something wholly and unnervingly different when they began to push themselves up and out of the ground by their roots. Their long, spidery legs peddled over boulders and across the detritus, impossibly transforming the forest before his eyes. Even as the trees crept around him, Patrick found his feet rooted—paralyzed with fear. Sweat beaded on his forehead and rolled into his eyes. His vision distorted and it became impossible for him to tell how near or far away things were from his groping hands as they hunted for a solid prop. His breath had become rapid and shallow, matching the dart of his eyes as he searched for some safe haven.

Without warning, a tree skulked over to him and took root. Unthinking, Patrick extended his hand, pressing a palm against the tree's bark to steady himself. He slowed his breathing and spotted a place to sit only a few yards away: a flat rock with a natural angle against which he could recline. With his hand still using the tree for support, Patrick tried to push his body toward the rock. Imperceptible to him, one of the púca—furious not only that Patrick had disturbed their structures, but also that he had not left an offering of those freshly picked blackberries—took his hand and steered him away from the stone chair and toward a stream flowing in the opposite direction. Patrick fell hard to the ground at the water's edge; his hands and knees sunk into the putrid mud. Hunched there, Patrick vomited up partially digested mushroom caps and blackberry bile.

Blaming his loss of equilibrium on food poisoning, Patrick slowly realized that his hallucinations were the result of haphazardly eating a misidentified mushroom. Now that he was becoming more lucid, if not sober, the trees had stopped rearranging the forest, allowing him to get his bearings. But the trees had moved, Patrick concluded. Or, at least, he found himself in a wholly unfamiliar place. How long, he wondered, was he under the spell of the mushrooms?

Too tired to carry on, Patrick pulled his limbs from the muck and rolled onto his back. Stars speckled the blackness above wherever there was a gap in the trees. Each time Patrick blinked his eyes wild trails of streaking light would hang before him and then disappear into the night. As he marveled at the night sky, the púca retreated into hollowed out trees, shallow burrows, pits, and caverns. Their eyes, however, remained fixed on two red orbs hovering in the far-away distance.

On the brink of sleep, Patrick rolled toward the stream to scoop a drink of water in his cupped hands. He rinsed the bile from his mouth and swallowed a few gulps before leaning over the current to splash his face. Just then, the swift-moving clouds parted for a moment, allowing the full brightness of the moon to shine upon the stream before eclipsing the light once again. At that moment, Patrick caught a fleeting glimpse of himself in the stream's reflection. His desiccated skin clung to his skull, sinking his eyes deep into their sockets. His cracked lips pulled tightly over his teeth, which threatened to break through the brittle flesh. His expression, contorted in pain, was eerily familiar to the Irishman.

Patrick scrambled away from the water, unsure of what he'd seen and unwilling to look again. He retreated to the low hanging branch of a nearby tree and hoisted himself up into the safety of its cradle. There he would try to sleep off the terrifying effects of those hallucinogenic mushrooms. The púca emerged from their shelters to gather around Patrick, now fully under the influence of their sinister magic. They whispered nightmares into his ears as he drifted into a drugged sleep.

Where the wandering water gushes
From the hills above Glen-Car,
In pools among the rushes
That scarce could bathe a star,
We seek for slumbering trout
And whispering in their ears
Give them unquiet dreams;
Leaning softly out
From ferns that drop their tears

Over the young streams.
*Come away, O human child!*
*To the waters and the wild*
*With a faery, hand in hand,*
*For the world's more full of weeping than you can understand.*

Patrick kneels beside his mother's bed clasping her skeletal hands in his own. He prays. His father, silent, lay next to her. Husband and wife share a bed in the far corner of the workhouse dormitory a few rows away from their children. The stone walls that surround them are slick with mildew. The stale air is difficult to breathe. Spiders crawl across their bodies uninhibited and spin their webs—like heartstrings—between the immobile parents. When Rory returns from the workhouse kitchen with a small bowl of oatmeal that the four of them are meant to share, Patrick refuses to eat his portion. He instructs his brother to eat and then insists that Rory spoon the rest into their parents' mouths. Having been through this before, Rory knows that his brother will not relent, and so he takes a bite of the brown paste, then raises the spoon first to his father's mouth, then his mother's. Rory lets the mush drop from the spoon to the back of their skulls. He looks at Patrick as he needlessly feeds their skeletons and says, "You did this."

"You did this," the priest hisses as he pulls shut the Iron Maiden's double doors, locking Patrick in the vertical sarcophagus. Short spikes—eight protruding from one door, thirteen from the other—pierce Patrick's vital organs, drawing forth streams of blood. The priest lingers before a slit in the device's mask to enjoy Patrick's cry of anguish and the look of pain that overwhelms his usually stubborn face. The priest smiles and then turns his attention to Kate, mother of his bastard son. He has stripped her of her clothing, bound her wrists and ankles with coarse rope, and thrown her to the blood-wet ground before the oozing Iron Maiden, forcing Patrick to witness her befoulment. Patrick locks eyes with Kate in an attempt to apologize for his impotence. Her glare refuses to absolve Patrick of his guilt. Though constrained, he cannot be compelled to watch—not again—and closes his eyes against the image of the priest disrobing. Kate, seeing that he has abandoned her, shrieks, "Curse you, Patrick!"

"Curse you, Patrick," Rory mutters as the noose is cinched around his neck. He is told to shut his mouth as a Pensioner Guard's fist crashes into his jaw, shattering it and his ability to speak. The other prisoners jeer from their cages at the captain as he descends the steps from the quarterdeck to oversee Rory's execution. The captain takes Rory's broken jaw in his hand and steers his chin until the two brothers are eye-to-eye. Patrick removes his bicorne and spits on his brother's face. "Rory Gallagher," Patrick begins, "As captain of the *Marion* and warden of her crew, I hereby announce your execution on behalf of Her Royal Majesty, Queen Victoria. Pursuant to the Bloody Code, you shall be hanged, drawn and quartered for bearing false testimony in an attempt to escape the life sentence handed down to you by the Irish Court of Exchequer. Let us pray for the salvation of this lost soul." At Patrick's nod, the executioner pitches the rope over a boom and hoists Rory into the air by his neck. As he thrashes, the rope is laid in a figure-8 pattern around the shipboard bitts mounted on the deck. Patrick watches with the disinterest of a stranger as his brother slowly dies of strangulation. Before the last flicker of life exits his body, Rory is taken down from the makeshift gallows, emasculated, disemboweled, and beheaded. His remains are then thrown into the ocean to chum the waters. The ship's fishermen stand on guard with readied harpoons. Rory's decapitated head sings to his brother as it sinks into the abyss, "Ee wahn chu, kyre." Patrick leans over the ship's railing to peer into the waters below. He is pushed from behind by an unseen hand and topples from the ship. As he splashes into the sea, he wakes from his unquiet dreams.

Patrick, having fallen from the bough of the tree, crashed unexpectedly into the unyielding dirt floor. He shook the memory of his nightmares from his head and rubbed at a strange burning sensation around his neck. Patrick could only vaguely recall the events of the previous evening but remembered the effects of the poisonous mushrooms. He retrieved the remaining caps from his sack and pitched them into a nearby bush. His eyes fixed on two, ripe Carmine Jewell cherries hanging from their stems like luminous red orbs. Patrick shook with dread.

> Away with us he's going,
> The solemn-eyed:
> He'll hear no more the lowing
> Of the calves on the warm hillside
> Or the kettle on the hob
> Sing peace into his breast,
> Or see the brown mice bob
> Round and round the oatmeal chest.
> *For he comes, the human child,*
> *To the waters and the wild*
> *With a faery, hand in hand,*
> *For the world's more full of weeping than he can understand.*

At the Port of Quebec, Patrick had been offered passage down the St. Lawrence river by a man named Owen Brown who was piloting a rabaska full of French firearms to a farm near Lake Placid, New York. Patrick had rowed in silence alongside ten other men, black and white. He had figured it best not to ask any questions concerning the assorted rifles and pistols lest he find himself without transportation. Once in Montreal, though, the men had secret business at some railroad depot that would delay their trip south a week, maybe two. Patrick elected to continue on foot as he hoped to reach New York City in time to send a letter to the Warden of the Port Arthur Penal Colony ahead of the *Marion's* arrival verifying his brother's innocence. After setting out on his own, Patrick had traveled south along the Richelieu River until marshland pushed him west into the mountains, which is when he began following the bent trees.

Unsure of where the previous evening's hallucinogenic nightmare had taken him, Patrick decided to climb above the tree line to get a better sense of his location. He scrambled up a section of exposed graphite that led him to a narrow ledge overlooking the Great Appalachian Valley. About a day's journey to the east Lake Champlain divided the Adirondacks from the Green Mountains of Vermont. "How did I manage to cover that much ground in one night?" he wondered. It was almost as if the wilderness had expanded while he slept, carrying him further from water's edge. There did appear to be a path through the valley back toward the lake, which, with any luck, would deliver him into the Hudson Valley and his new life as an Irish immigrant in New York City. Patrick paused on the ledge to imagine city life: music halls and public houses; manicured parks, and lazy seashores. He thought about sharing a pint with his brother once Rory straightened out the mess Patrick had gotten him into with the *Marion*. At this, though, Patrick's thoughts turned dark. He began to question whether his dream might have been a premonition and that his brother had been hanged.

"No," he said aloud, petitioning whoever might be listening. "It was just a dream." But the púca had returned. They emerged from burrows and scaled the rock face to surround Patrick on the ledge. Still, they remained somehow unseen. And as they goaded him with the priest's accusation—"You did this"— Patrick's thoughts turned somber. He took a step toward the edge. The voices in his head, those disembodied voices of the púca, convinced him that he was at fault for his brother's death and that the only absolution was to throw himself over the edge. Patrick took another step forward. He followed the faery voices, which had become increasingly articulate, "Ee wahn chu, kyre. We want you, here!" He stood at the precipice, prepared to plummet to his death, when a glimmer of light pierced his vision, interrupting the mysterious urge to jump.

Patrick winced at the intense glare. At first, he thought it was sunlight glinting off the placid lake water. But then it vanished. When the glare reappeared seconds later, he tried to locate its origin. The steady oscillation occurred for a couple of minutes. Then, the light stopped altogether. It was certainly unnatural, perhaps a signal of some sorts. Patrick shielded his eyes against the sun and scanned the near bank of the lake in an attempt to pinpoint the source. "Where?" Patrick breathed.

A conspiracy of ravens erupted from the still landscape of a small peninsula near the southern end of the lake. It drew Patrick's eye to a stone structure shrouded among overgrown trees. He was too far away to see it clearly, but when he squinted into the distance, he could tell that it sat atop a rocky outcropping high above the water. He thought perhaps it could be a lighthouse. The glare that had caught his eye could have been the keeper at work in the optics room. And, if that were the case, he might be able to labor for a meal and a night's rest—and maybe even secure passage down the Hudson River aboard a supplies ship.

Patrick eagerly descended the mountain, only to find that the forest had once again changed. A pair of thin waterfalls cascaded down a sheer rock face, into a jagged pool that wasn't there when he made his ascent. A stream flowed from the pool in the direction of Lake Champlain as if inviting Patrick to follow its course. Along the stream's northern bank a footpath had been beaten to ease his travel, while a low stone wall ran along the opposite side of the stream. Patrick could have almost described the new setting as charming except that an immense shadow had begun to inch toward him, blanketing the entire woods in unnatural darkness as it advanced.

He looked up to see what was eclipsing the sunlight, guessing it was nothing more than a storm cloud. He thought to find shelter from the coming rain but watched confused as the moon passed before the sun and impossibly stopped. Light and warmth were sapped from the forest. In the darkness, Patrick's hair stood on end. It was damnably cold. His breath rose in tendrils that lingered before him. He stared in disbelief as the condensation contorted into a cluster of fiendish faces, gnashing at him as if to eat his flesh. His hand swatted at the fog, causing the faces to recoil in torment before fading into nothing.

Patrick steadied his head with his hands and screamed into the void, "What is going on!" No echo returned. In fact, his voice hadn't made any sound at all. Frantic, he yelled again, "Hello?" He spun in circles looking for any sign of what might be causing this strange silence, which was exactly when he noticed that all the woods were completely mute. The tumbling waterfalls pounded silently against half-submerged boulders. The unrelenting swarm of black flies nipping at his gooseflesh produced no buzz. Patrick clapped his hands in an attempt to defy the hush. He felt them come together in a stinging strike but heard nothing. It was as if something had sucked the sound out of the forest.

Patrick let out a sob. His body stiffened. He couldn't force himself to move, and wouldn't know where to turn if he could. A wall of supernatural fog rolled toward him, pinning him against the stream. There was no option for retreat. Dim lights began to speckle the fog. They multiplied and brightened with each breath. "Will-o'-the-wisp" Patrick gasped. And for the first time, he saw the púca horde scuffling toward him, their faery fire blazing through the shadows. Patrick backed away until his feet were in the icy water.

He had turned to run when a high-pitched, guttural howl, as threatening as it was terrifying, ripped through the silence, stopping him cold. The force of the howl bent trees and knocked Patrick down into the stream. He scrambled to his feet and broke into an all-out sprint toward the lake. The sound of the púca rustling leaves and scattering stones close behind him drove Patrick forward. The sour smell of their breath turned his stomach, and the lure of their call—the same frightful phrases that Rory's decapitated head had sung to him in his dream, and that he had assumed were his own suicidal thoughts on the mountain ledge—curdled his mind.

Patrick wanted nothing but to be out of the forest, yet it felt like he wasn't making any progress. The fog kept pace with him, and the scenery remained the same. It was almost as if he was running in place. But then he passed something on the ground that he hadn't seen before. Patrick slowed down just enough to focus on the decapitated, 70-year-old skeleton of a Revolutionary War soldier, still dressed in his long-tailed coat of blue with red facing. A musket—with bent bayonet—lay nearby, clutched in a skeletal hand that had been ripped from its arm. The ribcage was splayed open as if something had tried to access the soldier's organs. Then, a second roar, more furious than the first, told Patrick the story of the soldier's fate.

The woods had thinned, and Patrick sprinted past three small gravestones worn smooth by two centuries of northeastern weather. He allowed himself to hope that these meant he was advancing toward the shelter of the structure he had spied from the mountaintop. And then, without warning, he emerged from the woods. Exhausted, Patrick instantly lost his footing and crashed to the ground. He stole a look behind him into the woods but saw nothing. Before him, the lighthouse loomed.

From the lantern room 30 feet above, the translucent figure of a woman dressed in a green, centuries-old gown watched Patrick's every move.

# 4

# Chapter Four

# Cloven Rock

His fists beat against the locked lighthouse door like a hail of cannon fire.

"Help!" he called. "Is anyone here?"

No one responded. He looked over his shoulder to see if anything had emerged from the woods and breathed a sigh of relief when he saw that he was still alone in the clearing. The faeries had been so close behind him that if they were able to leave the trees, they definitely would have surrounded him by now. He was less sure about whatever creature had made that awful growl.

"Hello?" He tried louder this time. "Please, let me in! Something's after me!"

There was no indication that anyone was going to open the door, so Patrick threw his shoulder into it. The door did not budge. A good sign, he thought, if he ever managed to get inside. He ran around the stone base of the lighthouse looking for another way in. At the backside of the structure, looking out over the barren lake, was a small, barred window. Heavy, drawn curtains obstructed his view of the interior. Patrick grasped the iron bars and shook furiously, to no avail. His only option was to scale the uneven limestone to the lantern gallery.

He quickly slipped his booted foot between the iron bars and began to hoist himself up the face of the lighthouse. A steady wind off the white-capped lake helped to pin him against the outer wall. He welcomed the assistance, as the stone didn't offer him any deep handholds. He held on with the tips of his fingers. The leisurely rhythm of the waves breaking on shore kept pace with the rise of his hands and feet. It was a precarious climb. Nonetheless, he managed to steadily drag himself up to the base of the gallery where his hands finally enjoyed a firm grasp on the baseboard. Patrick threw a leg over the edge and rolled onto the deck heaving a sigh of relief. He slowly flexed the tightness out of his fingers. From his newfound position of relative safety he allowed himself a peaceful moment for his muscles to recover from the arduous work. With his eyes closed, he listened to the *skwahck*-ing of seagulls overhead and basked in the heat of the sun warming his face. Patrick fell asleep.

The woman in green stood, unmoving, behind the lantern room window, studying the sleeping man supine on the gallery floor. Though her spectral face waivered in the light, her expression never changed. Like the Irish pirate queen, Grace O'Malley, the specter's long, orange hair framed delicate features and fell about her knees shimmering like Samhain bonfires. An unhealed gash had collapsed her left cheekbone into the crook of her nose, distracting from an otherwise handsome appearance. A constant effluvium of glistening ooze seeped from the festering wound. Despite this grotesque physical trauma, her wistful stare betrayed an even more profound psychological pain.

Patrick slept for hours. The sun set below the horizon, and its afterglow disappeared behind the mountains. When he awoke in the darkness, Patrick immediately scrambled for shelter. He pressed himself firmly against the lighthouse wall and searched for the creatures that had been in pursuit of him earlier that afternoon. It took his drowsy mind only a few moments to race through the events of the chase before it finally recalled the sanctuary of the lantern gallery, 30 feet above the forest floor. He relaxed; the woman watched.

The evening was pleasant, but Patrick wanted to get inside the lighthouse as soon as possible. He spun around and climbed to his feet in order to get a good look through the high windows. Unaware that he had come face-to-face with the woman's ghost, Patrick searched the lantern room. Curious that the beacon wasn't illuminated, nor did the clockwork mechanism work to turn the lamps. Surely this was the source of the glare he had seen from the mountaintop earlier in the afternoon: sunlight glinting off the reflective lenses as the mechanism spun about. Through the fixed window and across the gallery he spotted a rusted hatch in the parapet that would allow access to the interior lantern gallery. The woman's gaze followed as he made his way around the exterior to try the hatch. It was locked from the inside. Out of options, Patrick decided to smash a pane of glass. He looked around the gallery floor for something that he could use to throw against the window when, out of the corner of his searching eye, he saw that the ground-level entry door stood ajar.

"Hey!" he immediately yelled. "Up here!" Patrick half leaned over the gallery railing to get a better look, hoping that the person who must have opened the door would re-emerge and see him up above. "Hello!" he tried again when after a few moments no one appeared to greet him. Patrick began contemplating his ability to scale *down* the lighthouse wall. It was dark, but the moonlight shone just enough to illuminate the tricky descent. Before climbing over the railing, he scanned the tree line at the edge of the woods to make sure the púca were nowhere in sight. He hadn't seen or heard any sign of them since exiting the woods earlier in the afternoon, so he was hopeful that they had retreated into the depths of the forest in search of easier prey.

When still no one answered his call, Patrick swung a leg over the edge, then the other, and lowered himself slowly down. His feet searched desperately for footholds beneath him, while he clung as best he could to the limestone slick with evening dew. Throughout the gradual descent, Patrick darted his eyes between the wall before him and the woods behind him, fearing that at any moment some beast with ravenous red eyes would tear from the woods to pluck him from the wall. Two-thirds of the way down fear overwhelmed him, and he let go of the stones. He landed on his feet with a thud, but his knees buckled causing him to roll away from the structure and toward the woods. Patrick scrambled on all fours to the open door, and, without hesitation, lunged inside. He quickly slammed it behind him. The sound of metal smashing against the frame echoed eerily throughout the tower.

Patrick had walked through the doorway and the figure of the woman in green, who stood at the threshold upon his arrival. His movement dispersed her form as if he had walked through a cloud of smoke. She disappeared for only a few seconds while he wadded further into the room. When her figure came back together, it faced Patrick without having turned around. She observed him with the same unchanging expression as when she watched him sleep through the gallery glass.

Making a quick estimation of his new surroundings, Patrick called out again to the keeper of the lighthouse, "Hello? Is anyone here?" His voice echoed into the upper rooms following the path of the clashing metal. The state of the room in which he stood suggested nobody had occupied the lighthouse for decades, maybe longer. It's possible, he thought, that the lighthouse was not in service, but that someone had seen him milling about from the vantage of another lookout he hadn't been aware of and come to check on the property.

The room was dark, and Patrick had no way of illuminating it. In the blackness, he felt his way to where he estimated the small, barred window should be and drew back the curtain, allowing a flood of aurous light into the round, dusty room. It was a crudely furnished room, consisting of only a single wooden dining table and five matching chairs at the center. An unfinished beam of pine hung as a mantle above a scorched, brick hearth at the far end. He would have to collect some wood from the forest if he wanted to make a proper fire—a task he was not up to complete, especially in the dark. In the meantime, he tore the window curtain from its rod and wrapped it around the end of the wrought-iron fire poker, which he then lit into a torch with his flint and steel.

The miniature blaze revealed a roll-top desk near a stone

stairway which wound along the wall toward the upper floors. Curious, Patrick opened the desk releasing another cloud of dust. He choked and fanned his arms wildly about his face to clear the air before him. From the doorway, the woman continued to watch. When the cloud settled, Patrick lifted the lone item that was resting on the desk: a worn, leather-bound Bible. He instinctively scowled as the book reminded him of the monstrous priest. Patrick almost tossed it down without consideration, but his fingers felt an unevenness of the brittle pages which prompted him to open the cover. There, pressed between the cover and the first illuminated page, was a letter dated August 5, 1654.

Caleb,

During our travels throughout the Onondaga territory, we have discovered a salt spring located at the southern end of Lake Gannentaha. It was there we had hoped to establish a site for the French mission. We tested the water of the spring, which the Indians are afraid to drink, saying that it is inhabited by a demon who makes it foul. I found the fountain of salt water, from which we evaporated a little salt as natural as that from the sea, some of which we shall carry to Quebec. I have included among the enclosed supplies from the Plymouth Trading Company a small parcel of the Onondaga salt that Aoife might use for preserving your garden vegetables through the winter months. Blessings to the children.[4]

*Ad majorem Dei gloriam,*
Fr. Simon Le Moyne

"1654," Patrick said aloud while taking stock of the room, which began to look far more dated than he had initially bothered to notice. Two additional documents accompanying the letter informed Patrick that, at that time, a missionary shelter sat on the boundary line between Algonquin territory to the north and Iroquois territory to the south. It wasn't until the 1713 signing of the Treaty of Utrecht that control of the territories shifted to the French and the British respectively. By Patrick's arrival in the late-summer of 1847, the Split Rock lighthouse had only lighted the way for travelers upon Lake Champlain at the easternmost point of the Adirondacks for a mere decade.

His eyes were drawn to the darkness of the stairwell. The flickering light of his torch cast menacing shadows upon the wall that seemed to beckon him closer. Absentmindedly clutching the letter, Patrick followed the dancing light, making the climb to the first landing where Aoife's ghost was waiting for him. As he left the stairs, light from the torch illuminated what appeared to be a children's room. Aoife's expression, unchanged until now, winced at Patrick's intrusion.

Three small, neatly-made beds lined the wall opposite the stairs. A narrow shelf sat at the foot of each bed and contained one folded wool blanket and a toy. At the far left, five knucklebones lay atop the blanket. At the center, two stone spinning tops: one whipping top and one peg top. A doll made of leather and clay snuggled into the blanket on the final shelf. The room was otherwise bare, so Patrick turned to leave. He hesitated, though, recalling the three worn gravestones he had sprinted past in the woods. As if reading his mind, Aoife's ghost bowed her head in sorrow. Paused as he was at the center of the room, Patrick was able to see something lurking beneath the stairs. He moved forward to investigate but recoiled in horror when he got close enough to make out the shape of a horse's skull mounted upon a twisted tree branch. Shoved into each eye socket was a globe of red, blown glass that glowed in the torchlight. A strand of bells was strung around its neck with colorful ribbons, and a white sackcloth was draped over the upper portion of the branch. Once his initial shock had subsided, Patrick recognized it as a Mari Lwyd—a sinister hobbyhorse that was out of place amongst children's playthings. He hurried past it and up the next flight of stairs, to the second landing.

Again, Aoife was there to watch as Patrick violated the sanctity of her space with his very presence. She hovered beside a family portrait of a smiling husband and wife along with their three young children: two boys and a girl. The boys stood before their father, who had placed a proud hand on each of their small shoulders. The woman was seated in a crude chair but wore a beautiful green gown that was disturbingly out of place. The girl sat on her mother's lap cradling a baby doll in the crook of her arm. Beneath the painting sat an empty dresser; across from it, a large bed comforted and pillowed, beside which rested a prudent bassinet. Patrick peered inside and breathed a sigh of relief to find it empty.

He turned his attention to the ladder. It ran from floor to ceiling, leading up to a hatch that he thought must open into the watch room and then the lantern gallery above. His torch was nearly spent, so Patrick drew back the curtain covering the window to invite the moonglow into the room before climbing toward the hatch. At ceiling level, he found it padlocked, meaning that breaking in through the gallery window would have been useless. Naturally, he began wondering once again who—or what—had opened the entryway door granting him access to the interior of the lighthouse. Patrick stretched out on the plush bed to think. Aoife lay down beside him.

# Part II

# The Underground Railroad

# Chapter Five

# H(a)unted

On a bright winter morning—the kind that warms the soul following weeks of snow and ice whipping across the lake from Canada—Angèle Paris D'Arcantel walked from the woods carrying the decapitated head of a púca faery. Black blood dripped from its neck like syrup, painting a trail in the glistening white snow behind her. Patrick Gallagher looked up from his work, splitting firewood, at the sight of this unexpected figure approaching the lighthouse from the cursed woods. Angèle held up the head by one of its twisted horns and thrust it out before her as she would have a lantern to light the darkness. "Dis one got too close," she said to Patrick in a robust yet raspy voice. He had clasped his ax tight to his chest in a defensive position, unsure if he was next.

He used his free hand to shield his eyes from the sun-glare reflecting off the snow. When he saw exactly what Angèle was carrying, he let the ax drop to his side. "How?" he asked in a whisper of disbelief. Patrick had been living alone in the lighthouse for the previous six months, trapped between the bedeviled forest to the west and a three-hundred-foot basalt cliff to the east that plunged precipitously into the lake below. In that time, he had managed to get the lighthouse up and running—for the most part. Patrick had uncovered a pair of cellar doors, under some brush that had grown up around the base of the lighthouse, but, like the hatch leading up into the watch room, it was padlocked. Luckily, he found the keyring only a few days after he arrived. It was hidden in a box of letters that also contained a Claddagh ring and a diary filled with watercolor paintings.

The watch room was empty, but it did grant him access to the lantern gallery above where Patrick found barrels of paraffin oil and crates of phosphorus, which he used each night to ignite the lantern flame. He would then hand-crank the clockwork mechanism for three to four hours, sending an oscillating beam across Lake Champlain and over the dense woods. He hoped that it would alert a passing ship that the lighthouse was occupied and potentially in need of supplies. He never caught sight of a single ship, which was peculiar. He figured the lake to be a significant link in the shipping lanes that ran between New York City, Albany, Burlington, and Montreal. Once the lake froze over, he suspended the routine for fear of running out of oil.

There was no food in the cellar below, as he had feared. It was clear to him that the lighthouse hadn't been manned for some time. The last entry in the diary he had uncovered was from 1655, but it seemed absurd to think that no one had lived in that place for over two-hundred years. He had wondered who would have even built a lighthouse so long ago. Perhaps the Jesuit Missionaries—Father Simon Le Moyne, as the note he had found in the desk Bible suggested—constructed the tower as an outpost. But why had it been abandoned? Did something sinister really live in the woods? Patrick mulled these questions in his mind as he used the tools found in the cellar to ease his life at Cloven Rock. He set game traps; rigged barrels to collect snow, which he melted for drinking water, and filled the firewood piles with timber from outlying trees. He hadn't ventured back into the woods since his narrow escape.

Patrick was still unsure how the púca had come to be in the New World. He settled on a few theories. Perhaps Kate's curse had conjured them to stop him from arriving at his final destination or from reuniting with his brother. Another possibility was that they, too, boarded the coffin ships in Irish ports and lay hidden until they could escape into the North American wilderness where they would wreak havoc on a wholly new and unsuspecting people. Probably, though, he had imagined them. He had, after all, ingested a dangerous quantity of hallucinogenic mushrooms just before their appearance. But standing before him in knee deep snow was a woman, her skin as black as the blood that dripped from the creature's head, bearing proof that they haunted the inscrutable Adirondack forest.

"Who are you?" Patrick asked. "How did you get here?"

Angèle hadn't moved from the shadow of the trees when two brutes emerged from the woods behind her. They each exceeded seven feet in height, and their muscles bulged like the boulders upon which the lighthouse stood. Their faces were chiseled into expressionless, far-off stares. Neither one of them seemed to look at anything at all. They carried a large wooden chest suspended by a pair of poles that rested atop their massive shoulders. Whatever was inside that box, Patrick thought, was safe between the two guards. They stopped behind the woman as if their movement was predicated upon hers.

"I am Angèle. We came on the railroad."

Patrick was dumbfounded. "What railroad?"

"The one that runs underground," Angèle said.

Patrick had never heard of a subterranean railway and thought it strange that if one did exist that it would run through the North American wilderness and not beneath London or Paris.

"Is this a trick?" he asked. "What's in the trunk?"

"No trick," she said. The bushes behind her began to rustle. And though neither Angèle nor the brutes moved, Patrick raised his ax once again and warned them to get away from the woods.

"Come on." He motioned. "It's safe in the lighthouse!"

"I can see that," Angèle said. Her eyes had scanned the tower and spotted Aoife's ghost watching them from her perch in the lantern gallery. "It is safe here, too."

Patrick followed her gaze to the top of the lighthouse and wondered what it was Angèle saw that assured her of the tower's safety. His curiosity was interrupted when another three individuals exited the woods: two women and a boy. The women wore matching linsey-woolsey dresses and had wrapped their heads in red and yellow checked gingham turbans. The boy, aged about fourteen years, wore a livery coat, vest, a collared-shirt and pressed pants. His boots, though mucked by travel, were polished. They all looked scared. The women huddled beneath a single blanket, holding one another close, unsure if the clearing had delivered them from evil or if another trial awaited. The boy had pissed his nice pants.

"Cumberland," Angèle said.

"Yes, ma'am?" The boy asked.

"Rum," she said, stretching out her arm toward the boy so that he could place the bottle in her hand.

He loosened a sack from his shoulder and dropped it to the ground. Kneeling in the snow, Cumberland rummaged elbow deep for a bottle. Following a series of clanging sounds that indicated multiple containers of various shapes and sizes, he produced a clear, unmarked glass bottle half-filled with spiced rum. Cumberland placed it in Angèle's waiting hand, and she lifted the bottle to her mouth, set the protruding cork between her teeth and pulled it free. She then turned the púca's head over in her hands and filled it with rum. The alcohol seeped between bone and meat, diluting the creature's thick, black blood. When it began to overflow, Angèle returned the bottle to Cumberland, and, grasping the disembodied head by both horns, drank from it as if it were a sacred chalice.

Patrick's face tightened into a grimace. He clenched his jaw to make sure that the stomach bile filling his throat didn't escape. He choked it back down and continued to stare at the spectacle before him with confused disgust. The brutes remained unmoved, but the women had looked away. Cumberland cried.

When Angèle lowered the head from her mouth and smiled a toothy grin at Patrick, he gasped and took a step backward, thinking of retreat into the safety of the lighthouse. The púca's blood stained her teeth and glazed her nose and mouth and chin. Her eyes had rolled back into her head, and with the palm of her hand, she smeared the blood onto her cheeks and forehead as if painting a mask. "Rum," she demanded.

Cumberland again passed her the bottle, which she emptied into the púca's head. She then yelled into the woods, "Drink from the head of the pukwudgie, take it as if it were ours, and allow us to go on living!" With that, she threw the head back into the woods. With a sweeping gesture, she invited her companions to follow Patrick inside the lighthouse. Only, he didn't move. Even as the brutes walked past him without so much as acknowledging his presence; and then the women who offered him thankful, yet terrified glances; and, finally, Cumberland who looked more ashamed than anything, Patrick remained still. He hadn't taken his eyes off of Angèle.

"Who are you, Angèle?" Patrick asked.

"What is your name?" she said.

"Patrick," he replied.

"And how did you come to be here, Patrick?"

"On a boat," he said, mocking Angèle's brevity.

"Well, Patrick from across the sea, I will tell you my story. But it is long and unpleasant. Shall we first go inside?"

Patrick agreed, and as they walked together toward the lighthouse, he asked, "Do you know how the púca got here from Ireland?"

"Simple. Those are not púca," she said.

Patrick stopped and furrowed his brow. "Then what are they?"

"To be more precise, they both are and are not púca. The American Indians call them pukwudgie, and they are here now because they have always been here. My African ancestors might refer to them as tokoloshe. They are dark faeries, different only in name."

"And they leave you alone if you give them rum?"

Angèle laughed. "No, no. The pukwudgie are heinous. They want only to lure people to their deaths. They are also insatiable.

No matter how much food and drink you offer them, it could never be enough."

"I think they lured me here," Patrick said, motioning to the lighthouse.

"We shall see," Angèle said.

"So, the rum was for the thing that growls?" Patrick assumed.

"What thing that growls?" Angèle asked with a note of curious concern in her voice.

"You didn't hear it? I never got a good look—I think I caught it looking at me in the darkness. Its eyes glowed red," Patrick explained.

"Hmm, you are hunted?" Angèle said as if trying to make sense of this new development.

"Well, if you weren't offering rum to the pukwudgie or pleading with that other thing, then who were you talking to?" Patrick asked.

"Baron Samedi."

* * *

"Initially, there were nine of us," Angèle began. She and Cumberland, the two sisters—Mary and Emily—and Patrick all gathered around the dining table near the steady flames of the fire. Aoife sat not far away, in a padded chair by the hearth. She was knitting. After placing their wooden chest indoors, the two brutes had exited the lighthouse and stationed themselves on either side of the entryway door. Neither had spoken.

Patrick nodded his head at the group's dwindling numbers, "I'm the last of four that set out from County Cork last April."

"It seems we have all ended up in a place no less tragic than the journeys that have brought us here," Angèle observed.

"And those two?" Patrick motioned to the brutes guarding the door. "What's their story?"

"Darker still," Angèle admitted. "But let us begin at the

beginning."

"With Baron Samedi?" Patrick said. "Is he still in the woods?"

"No." Angèle smiled. "We must first begin with Papa Legba, for he is the Opener of the Way. And, yes, *he* is in the woods. But that is because *he* is everywhere, for the crossroads are everywhere."

Patrick looked at the other faces surrounding the table. They all stared back at him with solemn affirmation. "You mean he is your God?"

"No," Angèle said again.

"The Devil, then?" Patrick assumed.

"Papa Legba is the Lord of the Road, an intermediary between the lwa and the living."

"Lwa?" Patrick asked.

"Do not let these names confuse you, Patrick. Vodou is not a foreign story, but one that you will find to be intimately familiar. The lwa are spirits. Papa Legba is himself a lwa, but he is also the conduit between Guinee—the spirit world—and our own."

"Vodou," Patrick breathed. The word itself struck a chord of discontent. "So, he's some kind of Hades, a Lord of the Underworld?" Patrick asked.

Angèle shook her head. "No, no, no. The Baron controls Guinee. The Baron can be dangerous," she warned with a glance toward Aoife, who—being sensed—instantly disappeared from her chair. "Papa Legba, on the other hand, he is a paradox. He simultaneously removes obstacles while also blocking paths."

"How does that help us?" Patrick asked, his frustration mounting.

"Be calm. A door opened is a door closed. We appease Papa Legba so that he will allow us to speak with the lwa. We want to know what is that thing in the woods, yes?" Angèle said.

"Yes," Patrick agreed.

"Do not worry, you know of Papa Legba," she said to Patrick, who now looked even more confused. "You simply call him by a different name—Saint Peter, perhaps—much as you refer to the pukwudgie as púca."

"But—" Patrick began.

"Guinee is far less complex than our world, Patrick. We have complicated it by naming and renaming the lwa according to the hegemony: victors control our belief systems. Papa Legba has many names: Eshu-Elegba in Yorubaland, Eleggua in Cuba, and Exu in Brazil…"

"But—" Patrick continued, "St. Peter isn't real. There is no God of Abraham."

"Just as there are no púca?" Angèle said.

Patrick lowered his eyes. Angèle motioned to the sisters to fetch her bag. Emily retrieved it from beneath the table and brought forth from it a broad-brimmed straw hat, a corncob smoking pipe, and a weathered walking cane. She laid the items in her lap, waiting to see which of the persons in the room would request them. Meanwhile, Angèle had pulled a stick of white chalk from one of her pockets and began drawing a series of ornamental crosses upon the table.

"What is that?" Patrick asked.

"Papa's vèvè," Angèle said. "It is a beacon to let Papa know that we wish to speak with him and that we offer tobacco and rum." She lit three short, red candles, and rattled a calabash gourd covered in a loose web of beads and snake vertebrae. Small bells that were attached to the strings of beads rang a salutation. They continued to chime in concert with the percussion of the bones. She rose from the table and danced around it, spinning her white skirts and bowing toward the vèvè, singing.

*"Legba nan baye-a*
*Legba nan baye-a*
*Legba nan baye-a*
*Se ou ki pote drapo*
*Se ou k ap pare soley pou lwa yo."*

Emily, Mary, and Cumberland all began to pound out a simple rhythm on the table. The beat spread into the air of the lighthouse, echoing off the circular walls and up into the dark stairwell. Aoife had reappeared there to see what all the commotion was about. As she did, Cumberland stood up from his seat and began to dance around the table with Angèle. His movements, though, looked painful. His back became crooked, and his limbs twisted about in unnatural ways. When he came to Emily, he plucked the straw hat from her lap and placed it upon his head with a smile of thanks. Emily offered him the pipe and struck a match to light it. Cumberland gripped the pipe in his yellowed teeth and took a small puff. When he exhaled, an uncanny plume of smoke filled the room. He reached down for the cane, and when he stood up his hair had grayed, and he had sprouted a rough beard. Cumberland's eyes, though, remained youthful.

"Cumberland?" Patrick asked.

When the boy didn't respond, Angèle said, "Papa has mounted the boy." Turning her attention to the lwa, she spread her arms wide and said, "Papa Legba!"

He accepted her embrace, whispering into her ear, "So soon? What do you offer, this time?"

"Let me pour you a rum," she said.

"Mmmhmm," Papa Legba said, taking a jar of rum from Angèle. He spotted Aoife watching the ceremony from the stairwell and extended his hand to her, "Come in, child. Dance with us."

"Who are you talking to?" Patrick demanded.

Without taking his eyes from Aoife Papa said to everyone, "The Lady of the house."

"But there is no one here," Patrick said. "I've been alone ever since I arrived months ago."

"We are never alone." Papa Legba laughed and tossed back the glass of rum. "Don't worry, boy. She dead."

"Dead!" Patrick said, looking frantically for the woman's

ghost to appear. Aoife hadn't moved from the stairs. Tendrils of misty blood slowly cascaded from her wounded face down to the floor, where a pool had formed around her feet.

Angèle kissed both sides of Papa Legba's face and placed in his hands a carved wooden figurine. A child's toy. Papa grinned at the figure and slid it into Cumberland's shirt pocket. He patted the doll against his chest and asked Angèle, "What is our business this evening?"

"I'd like to know what hunts in the woods outside that door." She motioned to the lighthouse entryway.

He considered the portal, tipping up the brim of his hat for a better view. He raised his eyebrows at Angèle, though he said nothing. They all waited in the silence of the room. Papa Legba took another deep draw from his pipe. When he finally released the smoke from his lungs, he exhaled with it a single word: "Death."

"Could you be more specific?" Patrick asked.

Cumberland looked around the room frantically, unsure of where he was or if he might be in danger. Mary rushed to his side and held him tight while he regained his sense of place. His beard was gone, and his hair returned to its natural black color, prompting Patrick to wonder if it had all been an illusion.

"Is there a bed?" Angèle asked.

Patrick pointed to the ceiling without a word.

"Take him to rest," she instructed the sisters.

"What about my brother? What about Rory? Is he okay?" Patrick asked Cumberland.

"Papa Legba is gone," Angèle said. Mary and Emily ushered the boy past Aoife, who reached out a spectral hand to caress Cumberland's shoulder as he passed by her.

"Then bring him back!" Patrick demanded.

"It doesn't work that way, Patrick. We don't summon lwas. We entice them. Papa has other parties to attend," Angèle said calmly.

Patrick cursed. He blew out the candles, scattering wax and chalk dust in the process. He turned his eyes upon Angèle, holding her fast with his gaze. He muddled over in his mind the events of the day. He had seen her walk from the woods without a hint of fear. She drank from the head of a púca faery she claimed to have killed. She directed a pair of brutes as if they were golems rather than men. And she'd called upon a spirit to possess Cumberland.

Unsure what to make of any of this, but confident he would need her help if he were to escape the haunted lighthouse, Patrick asked once again, "Who are you?"

## Chapter Six

# The French Quarter

"Slave Dealing in New Orleans—An Auction"
*New York Tribune:* January 26, 1846
by NORTHROP

"Maria, step up here. There, gentlemen, is a fine, likely wench, aged twenty-
five: she is warranted healthy and sound,
with the exception of a slight lameness
in the left leg which does not damage
her at all. Step down, Maria, and walk."
The woman gets down, and steps off eight
or ten paces and turns, with a slight
limp, evidently with some pain, but doing
her best to conceal her defect of gait.–
The auctioneer is a Frenchman, and an-
nounces everything alternately in French
And English.

"Now, gentlemen, what is bid? She is
warranted—'elle est guarantie'—and sold
by a very respectable citizen. Two
hundred and fifty dollars, deux cent et
cinquantie dollars; why, gentlemen, what
do you mean? Get down, Maria, and
walk a little more; two hundred and
seventy-five, deux cent et soixante et
quinze, three hundred, troix cent—go on,
gentlemen! $325—trois cent et vignt
cinq, once! twice! ah! 350—trois cent
et cinquante; un fois! deux foix! going!

gone! For $350. A great bargain, gen-
tlemen."[5]

"On the day of my birth, and in the very same hospital, my father
was abducted and killed by a physician who then left on a ship
bound for London and disappeared from public record—so my
mother eventually told me. She carried me with her into the room
in which they had found him. His throat was severed down to
the spine by two cuts—one on either side of his neck. The lower
part of his abdomen was ripped open by a deep, jagged wound
and had been emptied of its organs. We were both smeared with
blood and smelled of rust and iron. She learned later that his
heart was missing. Apparently, the physician had taken it with
him. Thus was my introduction to the world.

"After that, my mother became a business woman out of
necessity. She imported liquor on Dauphine Street in the Faubourg
Marigny and supplemented her income by selling gris-gris bags
to French Quarter brothel workers and domestic servants as a
form of contraception. Our house always smelled of camphor oil
and fungus, and I could recite Psalm 44 word for word by my
fourth birthday. Rumor had it that Mama would attend to the
more salacious needs of higher-end clientele as well. Not directly,
mind you, but as an intermediary of sorts: love potions, spiritual
interventions, that kind of thing. As such, more than one attempt
was made on her life in hopes of keeping lecherous secrets from
being unearthed. In the wake of those attempts, Pere Antonio de
Sedella allowed her to conduct her rituals in his private garden,
behind the Saint Louis Cathedral on Royal Street. Of course,
Mama was always discrete. Though for our protection, Felicite
and I moved into our grandmother's rooms near Bayou St. John,
and Mama gave us new names lest some more desperate folks
got the idea they might use us for blackmail.

"In 1834, shortly after I had turned fourteen, my grandmother
was hired as a paid domestic servant at 1140 Royal Street, where

she worked as the personal cook for Madame Delphine LaLaurie. Felicite and I—at that time named Lia and Maria—moved into the house with our grandmother as *gens de couleur libres*. We were not, however, treated as such. Madam chained my grandmother to the kitchen stove by an iron clasp fitted around her ankle. On numerous occasions, Madam severely beat my grandmother because she had offered uneaten scraps of food to the LaLaurie's starving slaves. One night, my grandmother hid a note in Lia's turban—neither Lia nor I had learned to write—that detailed Madam's abuses. Lia was to deliver the note to Mama by passing it to one of the delivery boys. That evening, though, while Lia was brushing Madam's hair, she caught a frightful snag that sent Madam into a rage. She grabbed Lia's turban and pulled it from her head so that she could rip at my sister's hair in revenge. The concealed note drifted to the floor. That is when Madam LaLaurie reached for her whip.

"Madam had imprisoned me alongside my grandmother in the kitchen, but another of the chambermaids reported to me afterward that Lia darted between the fluted columns and through the ornamented double doors that led out to the balcony, tearing a heavy velvet curtain as she passed. Once on the balcony overlooking the intersection of Royal Street and Hospital Street, she climbed the iron stairs toward the roof. Incensed, Madam pursued her, screaming for Lia to return indoors to receive her just punishment. Those screams caught the attention of the LaLaurie's neighbors, who filed out onto their balconies to view the spectacle. Once Lia reached the roof, she would have looked out over the Vieux Carré to see the Mississippi River in its crescent before Jackson Square. It was from there, atop the cupola, that she plunged to her death while attempting to avoid the stinging lash in the hand of Madam Delphine LaLaurie.

"Before climbing down from the roof, Madam leaned over the edge to spit upon the disfigured corpse of my sister. Once back in the privacy of her home, Madam made her way straight into the kitchen where she confronted my grandmother about the note. She stuffed the paper into my grandmother's mouth and smacked her with the back of her hand: "Tonight you move to the attic for this insolence, and Lia's unpaid punishment will be wreaked upon you tenfold!" I heard the blow from my station at the washtub in the next room. But it was the threat that made me flinch. Those upper rooms, we all knew, were a torture chamber where Madam would stretch my friends upon racks for months until their limbs tore free from their bodies. All who entered that room died in that room—all except for Madam.[6]

"Fearing the unspeakable things that might befall her in those upper rooms, and unwilling to become another smell emanating from that attic, my grandmother instead resigned herself to death by fire. On April 10, 1834, she used the stove to which she had been chained to start a grease fire that quickly engulfed the rest of the house. At first, all I could smell was smoke, then the burning of my grandmother's hair, and finally her skin. It was so putrid that my stomach heaved. Had it even a morsel of food in it, I would have surely vomited it up. I wasn't chained to the sink, but the door between the washroom and the kitchen was barred. I was, however, able to contort myself through the pet-flap in the rear exit, which delivered me into the streets among the growing crowd. I didn't notice them at first because, crawling out of the house upon my hands and knees, I had come face-to-face with the broken body of my sister. After a moment, I reached out a hand to touch her, just to feel the skin of a loved one, even if it was cold and dead. But, before my hand made contact, I was pulled up from the street by my apron and hustled into a pen with the other servants that had managed to escape the inferno.

"At the front of the house, where Madam had managed to flee with her arms full of furs and jewels, but with none of her slaves to help her, the same neighbors who had watched Lia plunge to her death from the rooftop no more than one half of an hour earlier rushed into the fiery home to find the remainder of the LaLaurie's slaves. And they found them—in Madam's torture chamber. Corpses laid in heaps. Men were crucified on inverted tables, their eyes plucked from welted faces and hanging from the sockets, ears were cut clean, and the holes had been filled with their own excrement. Others were crammed into cages so small that their limbs had been broken and reset at odd angles. There were more stories flowing from the upper rooms and out into the streets, but I was taken away before I could hear them. I was confined in the Old Parish Prison on Orleans Street with nine other housemaids, where we were held until sold at auction. I had entered the LaLaurie mansion a freewoman and exited a slave."

\* \* \*

"I spent the following decade working as part of a labor gang at the Habitation Haydel sugar plantation. That was until Marcellin Haydel died and his widow, Marie Azélie, turned to industrial machinery that did not rely so heavily on human cogs. She got $350 for me last year when a Turk named Mehmed, claiming to be the Grand Vizier to Sultan Abdulmejid of the Ottoman Empire, purchased me at auction. He drove me by horse and gilded carriage to the Gardette-LePrete Mansion on Dauphine Street, back in the French Quarter, where I was initiated into the haram of a man said to be the Sultan's brother. He knew me as Maria; I knew him as The Turk.

"Everything in that house was false. I knew so immediately upon entering the great parlor. The first sound I heard was the clicking of a series of locks—too many, I had thought and wondered if they were meant to keep people in or out. I next noticed the group of musicians playing in a shadowed corner. Their music was peaceful at times, ecstatic at others. Their faces were masks of forced jubilance as they plucked at their instruments: a tanbur and kithara, a zither and ney flute. A singer chanted "Saba Peşrev" at The Turk's request. Despite their appearance and the tinkling sound of their music, a sadness hung in the air like the heavy tendrils of opium smoke that wavered in the lamplight. Across the room, through a dense throng of bare-chested dancers wearing only sheer, colorful skirts, was a large, plush bed accommodating a dozen or so writhing bodies. Writ large above the bed, spanning the entire length of the back wall, was a poem—untranslated from Farsi, and inked in blood:

از آ باز آ هر آنچه هستی باز آ گر کافر و گبر و بت‌پرستی باز آ این

درگه ما درگه نومیدی نیست صد بار اگر توبه شکستی باز آ

—جلال‌الدین محمد رومی. [7]

"Mehmed told me that the poem was wrongly accredited to Rumi, as the verse had been found among the papers of Abū-Sa'īd Abul-Khayr, who died 158 years before Rumi was even born. Though, of course, no one dared inform The Turk of his mistake. I did not mention to Mehmed that I could read the poem, having learned to read and write at Habitation Haydel under the tutelage of Anna, the concubine of Marie Azélie's brother, Antoine. She was a descendent of the Shirazi people, and so taught me the Persian language alongside English so that I would be able to recite properly gris-gris prayers of protection from the Quran.

"We waded into the sea of people on our way toward The Turk's bed, at the foot of which Mehmed lifted a long-stemmed pipe, with a beautifully ornate ceramic bowl, from a small lamp and offered it to me. When I declined, he thrust it at me angrily and demanded that I smoke it. More afraid of what might happen to me if I refused him a second time than if I ingested the drug, I lifted the pipe to my lips and sipped its milky smoke into my mouth. I held it there without drawing it down into my lungs. When I finally exhaled a yellow plume into the air, Mehmed smiled and said, "Good." He then undressed me and walked away with my clothes. I never saw him again.

"Uninterested in joining the orgy, and yet to be noticed by The Turk, I found a lounge near the vast central fountain where I could sit to conceal myself. From there I watched in dismay, especially the guards at each of the doors who leered at the women but remained steadfast at their posts. There were servants also: large, muscular men squiring platters of food and drink around the room to The Turk's guests. They, too, had been stripped of their clothing so that the guests could grope and fondle them as they pleased. The men never once looked directly at any other person in the room. They stared, as if in a trance, at the faraway walls.

"Two women sat down on the lounge next to me. They introduced themselves as sisters, Mary and Emily, originally from Plaquemines Parish. They told me that the entirety of the LePrete Mansion was opulent and that I would see for myself when taken to the private rooms upstairs. It was as if they were trying to distract me from what was coming by focusing my attention on the house rather than the people in it. A kind gesture, though unnecessary. I never left the parlor that night. But, if it was anything to judge the rest of the house by, there was no doubt of the luxuries—and the debauchery—that remained hidden to me.

"It was shortly after my conversation with the sisters that an air of nervousness suffocated the gaiety in the great parlor. A man, his long, white beard streaked with blood, staggered down the grand staircase and into the center of the room near the fountain beside which I had been sitting. Mary and Emily must have passed him on their way upstairs as they had recently been escorted from the lounge at the request of a delicate young man whose head was shaved bald. He wore garish purple robes and golden rings on nearly all of his fingers. He held out both of his hands, one to each of the sisters, which they accepted lest they suffer the consequences. And to me, he said, "Join us?" as if it were a question. One of the sisters whispered something in his ear, and he withdrew the invitation with a bow. "Please excuse me. Perhaps next time." I later learned from Emily that I had been spared a trip to the private rooms because The Turk had not yet taken me for his own, and his guests were forbidden from touching anyone that he had not first enjoyed.

"The old man who had descended the stairs, and now commanded the attention of most in the room, cradled in his arms the decapitated body of a naked child. When he opened his mouth to speak, instead of words a gurgle of blood erupted from the stump of his severed tongue, adding to the crimson stains upon his beard. The guards instantly drew their scimitars from their scabbards and looked seriously at the staircase. The music abruptly stopped, and all movement ceased. Laugher reverberated from the upper hall, rousing The Turk from beneath the pile of thrusting bodies heaped upon the enormous bed. Two eunuchs were quickly by his side with silk robes and a chalice of raki. He slipped into the robe as the other servant poured the drink into his mouth. The Turk then, with a flick of his chin, motioned for his personal bodyguard to climb the stairs. This man, charged with protecting a fraud, was so sure of his superiority that he hadn't even bothered to draw his weapon as he disappeared into the upper hall."

We waited.

"Every eye in that room was trained upon the balcony overlooking the empty staircase. We waited for The Turk's cavalier bodyguard to reappear and stride along the ornate Persian carpet pouring down each marbled step, his hand gliding softly along the golden railing that would deliver him back into the pit of delights. But, he never came, and would never come again. For it was my mother who appeared at the top of the stairs. And beside her stood the Sultan.

""Brother!" The Sultan boomed and spread his arms wide in mock salutation. "I see you are enjoying my women and my servants and my riches," he said while sauntering down the stairs.

"My mother, stoic, matched his pace. At the bottom of the stairs, they parted. The Sultan continued toward his brother, who had said nothing as he watched in disbelief; my mother came to stand before me with my clothes in her hands.

""Hurry, Angèle. We are leaving," Mama said.

"I dressed and embraced my mother, who I had not seen in years. She took my hand and led me toward the main entryway where we paused before a pair of The Turk's armed guards. Without turning around, and staring directly into the eyes of one of the guards who was unsure what to make of this development, my mother called out to The Turk's servants, "Absalom. Thomas." When the eunuchs left their post beside The Turk, a collective gasp filled the room, followed by frantic whispers questioning my mother's identity. Who was this woman, they wondered, that could command The Turk's personal servants? The two men stopped at the end of the bed where Mehmed had forced the opium pipe upon me. They brushed the lamp and pipe from the table upon which they sat and hoisted it onto their shoulders. It was then that I saw it was not a table, but a large wooden trunk. The Turk made a move as if he were going to try to stop them from walking away with whatever his brother had concealed inside, but the Sultan's assassins formed a wall around him."

""Abdulmejid!" The Turk begged.

""Silence!" the Sultan demanded. "Like a common thief, you stole from Topkapı Palace my brides and my treasures while I was attending the opening ceremonies of the Darülfünûn in Beyazıt Square. After months of searching, I have come to reclaim them.

""How did you find me?" The Turk asked.

""Did you even bother to open that sacred chest?" the Sultan replied.

""I would have gotten to it, once the rest of the money ran out," The Turk joked.

""No," the Sultan said. ""You would not have. For that chest is sealed by magic. It was my coronation gift from Pope Clement XII of the Catholic Church. And it is far more valuable than even you could imagine."

"Intrigued, The Turk asked, ""What is it?"

""Payment," his brother responded, "for bringing me your head."

"As I watched the brutes lumber across the floor, the sisters had reappeared at the top of the staircase among a small crowd spectating the scene. I placed a hand upon my mother's shawled shoulder and pointed to the sisters. I related to her their gesture of kindness, which she rewarded with a nod. I waved them to us, and though they hesitated for a moment unsure of my mother's authority, both were soon running down the stairs towards what they hoped would be their freedom.

"My mother took a step closer to the guards that were blocking our path with their swords. "Let them pass," the Sultan shouted, and The Turk's guards, to his dismay, stepped aside.

"Before exiting the mansion into the humid New Orleans midnight, my mother issued a command to the Sultan.

""Kill them all."

"When the door shut behind us, I once again heard the clicking of too many locks being bolted shut and knew, then, that they had been installed to keep everyone in."

* * *

"The following morning we were afloat upon the Mississippi River, nearing Baton Rouge, with our sights set on Cairo, Illinois, when a young man—out for his morning constitutional—came across a very different sort of river flowing from beneath the doors of the Gardette-LePrete Mansion. I had agreed, at my mother's request, to accompany Absalom and Thomas, along with Mary and Emily, to the confluence of the Mississippi and Ohio Rivers where they would then catch a ride on the underground railroad to Nova Scotia with a man named John Brown Jr. who conducted the route between New Orleans and Put-in-Bay.

""War is coming," Mama had said at the dock, ""and the South is poised to rise like snakes from their January slumber, to strike with their poisoned fangs the heels of those who would dare tread upon them."

"When I asked her if she meant that as a warning or a threat she replied, ""Both."

"The man stopped when he noticed a thick stream of blood oozing from beneath the door and down the front steps of the Mansion. It pooled in the crevices and cobblestone divots of the uneven sidewalk, until finally spilling over into the sloped streets. Not the least bit curious, he turned and ran three blocks to the nearest police station where he related to them between gasps for air what he had seen. When the police arrived at the Mansion gates, detectives found them unlocked. Similarly, all of the doors and windows had been unlatched. Inside, the carnage was nearly unbearable. Mutilated bodies littered the ground and hung from the chandeliers. On the large bed, dismembered corpses clutched at one another. The air was infused with a sickening metallic aroma. Detectives followed the trail of gore through the house and out into the courtyard where, earlier that morning, rain had washed through New Orleans from the Gulf of Mexico turning the flower beds into mud troughs. From one of the muddy pools a single hand, frozen into a lifeless claw, protruded from the ground like the Devil's Hand flower.

"The Turk had been buried alive. A mob of footprints in the wet ground suggested that the Sultan and his assassins waited for The Turk to suffocate before they departed. It seemed as if they had covered him in a grave just shallow enough to ensure that in his final moments he might feel the fresh air of freedom within his grasp, only to suffocate an arm's length below the sodden earth."

# Chapter Seven

# Denial

"You've made it quite a bit farther north than Illinois," Patrick stated.

"We have," Angèle agreed.

Mary and Emily returned from the upstairs where they had put Cumberland to rest in the master bedroom on the third floor. "He seems alright," Mary assured the others, "just tired." She poured herself a dram of rum, then offered the bottle to her sister, who took a swig from the dregs.

"He'll be fine," Angèle said, "Papa Legba does not wish to harm him. Kalfu, maybe, but not Papa."

Patrick groaned at the mention of another unknown entity. "Who is Kalfu?" he asked.

"Something of an evil twin, but not quite," Angèle said.

"And when does he show up?" Patrick asked.

"It's not likely that he will, so you can rest easy," Angèle assured him. She then turned to Mary and Emily to say, "I was just telling Patrick of our journey up the river." The faces of both women darkened.

"Are you sure?" Emily asked Angèle.

"He should know," Angèle said.

"Know what?" Patrick said.

"Angèle," Mary protested.

"Know what?" Patrick demanded.

"We have all of us walked through the fire," Angèle said to the group. "The flames that licked at the heels of some were hotter than those that snipped at others. But we have all of us been scorched nonetheless."

"What are you talking about?" Patrick said. He slammed his hand down on the table.

"I'm talking about escape," Angèle declared.

"And how do you propose we slip past that thing lurking in those woods out there?" He waved a finger frantically. "Is your mother going to show up to shepherd us through that nightmare?"

Angèle's eyes flashed, and he quickly regretted what he had said. Patrick looked away from the three women sitting across from him. His thoughts turned to Kate, and his inability—or worse, unwillingness (he couldn't be sure)—to put an end to the abuses imposed upon her by the priest. Patrick had feared him as he now feared the forest.

"There are ways out of the sturdiest prisons," Angèle said. "Even the Devil can beat his wings and fly free from Hell."

Patrick lifted his eyes and looked at her with wonder.

"We seen him in Cairo," Angèle said.

* * *

"The thing about Cairo is that be it as it may a geographically northern town, that don't stop it from being a place mentally and spiritually as southern as New Orleans or Tuscaloosa. So, we had been instructed to meet Mr. Brown near the gasworks, which sat east of Commercial Avenue, nearest the riverbank— the idea being to slip in and out under cover of night without attracting any unwanted attention, if you catch my meaning. Mr. Brown, you see, was to take us by steamboat as far north as the Erie Canal.

"When we finally arrived in Cairo, it was impossible to see anything from the water. A perpetual and impenetrable fog shrouds that sunken peninsula. Fortunately, for us, that meant that it was equally unlikely that anyone had observed our arrival. Or so we had foolishly assumed. We moored our flatboat among the trees growing up out of the muck as there wasn't any place you might call a landing. Absalom and Thomas were first out of the boat. The frigid water reached up to mid-thigh on each of the giants, which would have put the sisters and me more than waist deep. I jumped in while Mary climbed upon Absalom's back and Emily upon Thomas's. Together we carefully scrambled up a steep embankment and over a levy wall before catching sight of the town. The sisters were hoisted over the wall first, then me. Absalom and Thomas followed. Once on the other side, we kept strictly in contact with the levy as Cairo had no street lamps and the new moon shed no light in the clouded night sky. The darkness was so complete that I could not even make out the shape of Thomas mere inches in front of me. Still, something followed us; we were being hunted.

"Our small group slunk along the vast wall for no more than a quarter mile, though that unshaped blackness felt interminable. Try as I might, I could not create a sensation of space and began to feel an overwhelming sense of agoraphobia taking hold. The tips of my fingers had rubbed raw from running them along the rough concrete in order to keep some physical contact in the dark. And just as my hand dropped from the wall in pained desperation, Thomas reached back to alert me to the sight of a beautiful, orange flicker shining forth from a short candle in the basement window of the gasworks.

"In hushed whispers, we affirmed the presence of everyone in our group before setting out into the terrible void. Closer and closer we crept toward the candlelight. With each step, I grew more anxious, but that light was the sign Mr. Brown had promised as our beacon of salvation. When we finally arrived at the building, Absalom rapped on the cold, smooth window to alert Mr. Brown of our arrival. Immediately, a hand reached out into the darkness and gripped Absalom tight by the wrist. Startled, Absalom swung his arm in a full arc, guessing at the location of the hand's owner. His fist crashed into an unseen face, which let out a cry of intense pain. We were all too stunned— and, admittedly, afraid—to flee. Even if we had run, we wouldn't have got far. Absalom's accoster was not alone. From behind the building a fugitive slave patrol of about a dozen men, armed with torches, whips, and guns emerged to surround us. We must have been lured there by a false promise. I questioned whether Mr. Brown was even a real man, or a character devised to trick runaways into the snares of bigotry.

"The slave patrol asked no questions. In fact, I cannot recall anyone speaking a single word before or after the noose was strung around Absalom's neck. Thomas was next. Someone else worked to bind my wrists and ankles in heavy shackles and then secured me to Mary with an arm's length of chain. Mary was similarly bound and yoked to Emily. For a short while, the only sound any of us heard was the rattling of our chains as we were forced to shuffle our way two blocks north along Fourteenth Street, to the custom house. Only the torchlight and then the snap of whips stinging the backs of Absalom and Thomas guided us. Soon, though, the jeers of a seething mob reached our ears, even before the light from their bonfires illuminated the scene. The scent of burning leaves and smoldering logs filled our noses with a velvety smoke that tricked our minds into feeling a metaphysical warmth despite our soaked clothes and the icy grip of inescapable death—a strange preamble of comfort to the horrors ahead.

"A crowd of about two hundred men, women, and children had gathered at the town center to witness the lynching of a man named James Williams, who stood accused of murdering a young white girl. Her body had been found in a pond behind the schoolhouse after it had gone missing some days prior. The authorities saw no sign of struggle nor abuse that would indicate foul play of any kind, but the town wanted someone to pay for the tragedy. It was likely that the girl was playing alone near the water's edge and simply fell in. And with no one around to help her to the shore, she probably panicked and drowned. Mr. Williams had said as much as he endured their vicious beatings. He even denied the charges after the mob tarred and then feathered him in hopes that the humiliation, if not the pain, would elicit a confession. Unpersuaded by Mr. Williams's claims of innocence, the mob hung him from the archway above the intersection of Fourteenth and Poplar streets. It was a band of women who were first to pull the rope, so outraged were they at this loss of a child, and so afraid for the safety of their own daughters. With the furnace of their racial hatred stoked by delusions of righteous indignation, the fates of our friends, Absalom and Thomas, were sealed."

"How did they escape?" Patrick interjected.

"They didn't," Angèle said.

Patrick's jaw slackened, he could find no words to object, even as his mind denied what Angèle had just said.

"They beat those two men within a breath of their lives, and—mistaking Mary and Emily for their wives—demeaned them in ways that would have made Madam LaLaurie blush. I remained chained to them through it all and took a few beatings of my own, though I was spared the worst of it. Why I cannot be certain. I think because the mob took more pleasure from forcing Absalom and Thomas to watch their supposed brides violated than from the actual defiling itself," Angèle reported.

It was a question Patrick had often asked himself about the priest who had offered him a malicious grin upon being caught in the act of raping Kate. He tried to banish the vision of that devilish face from his mind and said, "But, I watched those two walk out of the woods. They're standing guard on the other side of that door right now..." Patrick trailed off as he realized that Absalom and Thomas had indeed been posted outside for hours in the darkness, exposed to the bitter winds that whipped off the frozen lake, which Patrick had found he could only endure for mere minutes before having to retreat inside to the warmth of the hearth fire.

"You're not wrong," Mary said, casting an ornery look at Angèle.

"Well, then, what happened?" Patrick asked.

"The mob strung them up next to James Williams's corpse and watched with excitement as their bodies struggled against suffocation. The children cheered the loudest. When each of the men had stopped moving, the mob fired their guns at them—"Best to make sure," I heard someone say. From further away, a young man threw a torch that soared above the mob like a comet before igniting Mr. Williams's tar-coated body. The crowd's delight was deafening. Eventually, though, their celebration died down, and the people of Cairo congratulated one another and dispersed back to their homes. A deputy locked our chains to the base of the archway from which Absalom and Thomas hung. We were told that the sheriff would be by in the morning to transport us to the auction house or the morgue—depending.

"It was so very cold. The three of us huddled together for warmth as best we could, but our body heat did little to stave off the winter's bite. We cowered in the darkness for more than an hour before the sound of hushed footsteps patting on the dirt road broke the silence. They advanced at a slow and irregular pace, but we could tell from the tone that the footsteps belonged to a single person. It was too early to be the sheriff and probably too late to be someone from the crowd returning to inflict more pain. With no other option, we—the sisters and I—held each other tight.

"The footsteps approached us from behind, so we couldn't see the stranger until he knelt down beside us. The man held a small candle in a brass saucer that illuminated his bearded face. The first words he spoke were an apology.

""I'm sorry about all this, and about the wait. I had to be sure no one was standing guard or lingering nearby."

"He covered Mary and Emily with wool blankets and set to work picking the lock that bound us to the arch.

"John Brown?" I asked.

""No, Ma'am," he said, "that'd be my father. You can call me

Junior. Really, again, I'm very sorry for the delay, but I had to be sure no one was watching. I was sequestered in the gasworks when I heard word that a lookout from the Missouri side of the river had spotted you approaching Cairo and tipped off the FSP boys to your whereabouts. They were on your trail as soon as you ran your flatboat ashore. If I had left to warn you, we'd all be dead right now."

"He worked free the lock securing us to the archway and set to removing the shackles from our ankles. It was slow work by candlelight, and the cold made it significantly more difficult.

"Once our legs were free Junior suggested we run to the steamer waiting for us on the Ohio River not far from where we had hidden our flatboat. Those are our men up there, I told him.

""I know, Ma'am," Junior said.

"Well, we are not leaving them swinging there like rotten fruit."

""What would you have me do? There's no time to bury them. We've got to get to the steamer. There are others waiting for us," Junior said.

"Cut 'em down," I ordered.

"Junior, seeing that I would not budge from this position and that Emily and Mary were in agreement with me, looked up and down the street to make sure we hadn't attracted any unwanted attention. He then handed me his torsion wrench and ball pick."

""See what you can do."

"With that, he began scaling the arch's wrought iron lattice.

"I didn't know how to operate the tools, so I fished around inside the locks binding our wrists without any luck as the bodies hit the ground with two successive thumps. The sound gave me a start, and I fumbled the tools. When I picked them up my face turned to look at those innocent men. It wasn't until I saw them lying there, broken and bloodied and covered in ridiculous feathers that I said—No!—denying the fact of their death. Mr. Brown tucked his knife back into his waistband and hung from the apex of the arch by his fingers before letting go to land next to the bodies he had cut free.

"A faint purplish light began to sprout from behind the seemingly endless rows of corn stalks lined neatly, like well-drilled soldiers, upon the Kentucky farmland across the wide river. In a few more minutes, the sun would break the horizon and wash us in the golden glow of dawn. "We've got to get out of here, now," I said.

""Agreed, let's move," Juinor said.

"I handed him the lock-picking tools and helped Emily to her feet.

"We're gonna have to drag them."

"Emily looked at me with disbelief.

""We can't move them like that. We need a cart or something."

"No time to find a cart, I said. And with my wrists still shackled in the iron cuffs, I picked the rope up off the street and slung it over my shoulder. Grab the end and pull.

"Emily did as I asked and we began our tramp toward the river. Junior and Mary followed with Absalom in tow.

* * *

"Junior returned to our makeshift shelter on the river carrying the supplies I had asked him to gather, while Emily, Mary, and I prepared the bodies. We first removed the nooses from their necks and tied them to their waists. Then we secured the free end of each rope to a sturdy tree near the water line so that the bodies wouldn't float away as we plucked the feathers and scrubbed the tar from their flesh. We next hoisted them up out of the water and laid them down on the steep embankment and covered them in a thin layer of mud that quickly dried and chalked their skin, marking them for the Guédé. Finally, we slathered ourselves with sludge from the river and waited for it to dry. The sun had risen above the fields to the east, and its rays stretched out across the water, warming southern Illinois. The river cooed a peaceful melody that we might have enjoyed if our skins were a different color. As it were, we were on the run, and each moment we waited on that riverbank the more unlikely our escape became.

""Coffee, roasted peanuts, cigars, and bourbon," Junior reported.

"Bourbon?"" I asked, doubtful.

""I don't think there's a single bottle of rum within a couple hundred miles of this town," Junior said.

"And the rest?

"Junior pulled a rooster from the sack and held it up by its legs.

""One live chicken."

"I nodded"". Let's get to work.

""You had better be quick," Junior pleaded. ""If any of the townsfolk catch up with us I'll be in more trouble for stealing this bird than the bodies of those runaways."""

"Before Junior finished speaking, I had already begun drawing in the dirt. Mary and Emily initiated their wild dance in the water, knocking together smooth river stones to keep a rhythm. I selected from my small collection of holy cards the image of Saint Lazarus of Bethany and laid it down on a piece of red cloth cut from one of the blankets Junior had given the sisters. I offered Papa Legba one of the two cigars Junior had procured, along with a handful of peanuts, and lit the stub of the white candle we had first seen in the gasworks window.

""What are you doing?" Junior asked.

"Asking Papa for permission to speak with the Baron, I explained."

""I thought we were burying your dead—quickly!" Junior said.

"They are not yet dead irretrievable. We will ask Baron Samedi to reject their spirits, I said."

""Those men are dead, Angèle. What you're saying is impossible," Junior argued.

"*Legba nan baye-a*
*Legba nan baye-a*
*Legba nan baye-a*
*Se ou ki pote drapo*
*Se ou k ap pare soley pou lwa yo.*

""Your spirit likes to smoke and eat peanuts?" Junior questioned.

"The lwa do not need food, but we offer them these sacred items so that they may transform them into energy that manifests our petition in the physical world, I explained, ignoring Junior's dismissive tone.

"Nothing happened, at least as far as Junior could tell. But, Papa would open the gate. I uncorked the bottle of bourbon and poured it three times on the ground, then repeated the process with the jar of black coffee. We each took a swig from the bottle of bourbon to warm our bones and to participate in the celebration aimed at attracting the Baron's attention. I then lit the remaining cigar and puffed at it until a cherry ripened at its end. I smoked while drawing the Baron's vèvè in the dirt: a grave marked with a cross and flanked by two caskets. I placed the smoldering cigar across the vèvè and called out to BaronSamedi.

"Lord of the Cemetery! Mighty Judge and Healer! Please come and accept these offerings! With a broken shard of glass collected from among the detritus left behind by receding river waters, I slit the chicken's throat allowing its blood to spill out over the vèvè. Each of the sisters stepped forward in turn, with their hands cupped before them. Blood poured into their hands, and when they had each collected enough, we masked our faces in crimson. Mary and Emily each kissed the forehead of Absalom and Thomas, smearing them with the muddied blood of our sacrifice in the process.

"I removed the lid of a wax-sealed glass jar that contained within it a noxious white powder that I then carefully sprinkled on the blood-smeared forehead of both men. I used very little, merely a dusting, for it was made from the dried reproductive organs of the poisonous puffer fish. The powder also included the crushed skull of a deceased infant, blood from a freshly killed blue lizard, the ashes of a cremated toad that had been wrapped in a dried sea worm, and a few fibers of itching pea.

""What is that stuff?" Mr. Brown asked.

"Zombi powder." I replaced the lid with the same care I had taken to remove it and packed the jar away in a series of intricate wrappings. The sisters continued their erratic dance as quietly as possible in the ankle-deep water surrounded by piles of brush.

""What is a zombi?" Mr. Brown asked.

"I didn't answer, hoping that the Baron would grant our request to reanimate Absalom and Thomas, and therefore allow Mr. Brown to see for himself.

"When I wasn't forthcoming with an answer, he pressed, ""Is this witchcraft?"

"Not exactly, I said. The sisters and I quaffed from the bottle of bourbon—even Mr. Brown took a mouthful—and chewed the glass once the final drop had been swallowed.

"The sun was higher, and we still had a ways to wade along the shoreline before reaching the relative safety of John Brown Jr.'s steamboat. I could see the worry settle into Junior's face. His jaw clenched and unclenched, counting the seconds that slipped by, anticipating any sign that might get us moving. Whether he was expecting to be caught or for the men to spring to life, I couldn't be sure. His eyes scanned the river—up and down, up and down, up and down—then he would peek his head over the embankment in a series of three, long glances to see if anyone was coming. Then he would return his eyes to the river—up and down, up and down, up and down. Finally, when he could take our inaction no longer, he demanded that we leave the men behind lest we face our own certain deaths.

""There are others on the boat who have trusted me with their lives. I plan on delivering them to my terminus and safely transferring them into the custody of the northeast conductor. I'm leaving. Now!""

While Junior was delivering his speech to the three of us dancing in the river, Thomas had stirred, opened his eyes, and stood up. Absalom then struggled to his feet next to him. Neither man wore any expression. They both stared directly at me, as if they were waiting for a command. So, I asked them to fetch my wooden trunk from our flatboat and to carry it to the steamer down the shore.

"Okay, Mr. Brown, I said, lead the way.

"Junior looked at me in full denial of his own senses. ""I don't believe it," he said."

8

# Chapter Eight

## Keening Banshee

"I'm not sure I believe it either," Patrick admitted.

"Yet you said yourself that they walked from the woods under their own power," Angèle objected.

"That doesn't prove that they died and you brought them back to life," Patrick countered.

"I didn't bring them back to life. Baron Samedi refused their souls at my request, which allowed them to return to their bodies," Angèle clarified.

"All I'm saying is that your story doesn't *prove* that those men died in Cairo," Patrick said.

"But they did," Emily protested. "Tell him, Mary. You saw it too."

"That's right. Everything Angèle has told you is true," Mary confirmed.

Angèle could see that Patrick was not persuaded. "You were witness to Papa Legba's possession of Cumberland."

"An act," Patrick said, fed up with her fabrications.

"But why, Patrick? What do we have to gain by fooling you?" Angèle asked.

"I don't know," Patrick said. "Maybe you want to frighten me so that I'll leave this place. Maybe you want to live here by yourselves, safe from the horrors of the world. But you've made a mistake; the woods are far more frightening than your stories—I'm not going back in there."

"We don't want to stay here. Our families are in Nova Scotia," Emily said.

"And we lost people in those woods too!" Mary insisted.

"Did you?" Patrick asked, curious.

"Of course we did! You are not the only one who is afraid," Mary said.

Angèle took a deep breath. "You encountered the pukwudgie in the woods as well as something you've claimed is worse still. Those creatures are real, Patrick. The lwa exist. Those men outside—bruises around their necks and riddled with bullet wounds that you can inspect for yourself—walk because life pulses once again through their veins. And still, you disbelieve?"

"I don't know! This is madness!" Patrick cried.

"You'll need to trust us if you want to escape this prison," Angèle stated. "And we'll need your help if we are to have any hope of escape. We don't know what we're dealing with out there, but you've seen it, even if only from afar."

At that moment, more confused than he had been in a long while, Patrick bowed his head and prayed. The knuckles of his interlaced fingers turned white from the force with which he squeezed them together. He had given up the practice when his prayers of desperation had gone unanswered from within the Iron Maiden, where the priest once locked him in the basement of St. Joseph's Chapel to watch as he abused Kate. Patrick had cursed Ireland's uncaring God and turned his back on the Roman Catholic Church.

"Not everything is so unbelievable, then?" Angèle said, a wry smile distorting her lips.

"It's just habit. I don't actually think anyone is listening," Patrick confessed. He lifted his head and looked at the women sitting across the table from him. He forced himself to consider their stories as true—the unrelenting psychological, emotional, and physical pain that they would have endured made his head spin. "Maybe we could survive here forever," he began. "Maybe life would even be bearable, hidden away from the insatiable appetite of civilization that wants only to use us as fuel for its own growth—"

Angèle sucked in her breath as something Patrick had just said gave her an idea.

"—But, I need to find my brother who, at best, is rotting away in an Australian penal colony because of me," Patrick continued. "To do that, I have to get off this split rock and down to New York City. So—"

"Patrick!" Angèle interrupted.

"What?"

"What did you see in those woods that frightened you so?" Angèle asked, studying his face.

Persuaded by her inquisitive tone, Patrick answered, "Strange things, as if a waking nightmare. Reality became unreal."

"Yes, but what, *exactly*, did you see," Angèle pressed.

"There was this pair of devilish red orbs. Eyes, I'm certain, that glowed at me from far away. As shocked as I was, I almost wanted to go to them. Their unblinking stare lured me at least a few paces closer, I remember. But then it growled—no ordinary growl. As the creature drew in its breath, a supernatural wind pulled me ever closer to it. I grasped at branches to slow my progress. It sucked all sound from the woods as if it had left a hole in the world."

"What do you mean?" Angèle asked.

"I mean nothing made any sound, including me. I screamed, but heard nothing," Patrick said.

"Curious," Angèle said. "I've never heard of anything like that before."

"That isn't the least of it; there were stranger things still. Such was the power of its breath that streams reversed their course, flowing in the opposite direction. And when it finally did bellow forth its rage, a fierce wind snapped trees in half and sent rocks the size of my head—and bigger—rolling along the forest floor like dried leaves drifting on a cool autumn breeze."

It was Emily and Mary's turn to doubt. "That's impossible," they said almost in unison.

"I know!" Patrick said.

"Then what happened? Did it pursue you?" Angèle asked.

"I'm not sure. I ran as fast as I could. The púca chased me;

of that I am certain. They almost surrounded me, too, what seemed like hundreds of them. But then I stumbled from the woods near the exact spot you all exited, into the shadow of the lighthouse. I scrambled toward the building, but nothing followed. Thankfully, too, because the door was locked," Patrick said.

"How did you get in?" Emily asked.

"I climbed to the gallery thinking I might be able to pry open a window, or at least smash one, and while I was looking about for something to use to bust the glass, I noticed that the front door had opened," Patrick said. "I figured the keeper had returned, or at least decided it was safe to investigate the commotion I was making."

"So, who opened the door?" Emily asked.

"That just it, I don't know," Patrick said.

* * *

Cumberland awoke from his slumber in what had become Patrick's bed and followed the sound of voices toward the bottom of the spiral staircase. He could smell chestnuts roasting on the fire, and his stomach rumbled in anticipation. At the bottom of the stairs, he emerged from the stone stairwell rubbing the sleep from his eyes. "Sorry everyone, I sure was tired," he said to the group sitting around the table. Cumberland sat down upon the empty chair and reached a hand toward the dish holding the chestnuts.

Patrick slid him a plate piled with roasted seagull and Cumberland smiled his thanks as his mouth was already stuffed.

"Did you sleep well?" Angèle asked.

"Yes, Ma'am. Must have been the fright of running through those woods," he said with a yawn, "but I haven't been that dead-to-the-world since before we left Nashville." He studied the mess upon the table as he talked: a distorted chalk drawing, candle wax splattered across it, and an empty bottle of rum. "So, did we speak with Papa?"

"You don't remember?" Patrick asked.

"Not really," Cumberland said.

"Yes," Angèle answered the boy.

"Is he going to help us?"

"It was more of an information session," Angèle said.

"Yeah, but we learned what we already knew. 'Death' is in the woods," Patrick informed Cumberland.

"We were just about to tell Patrick of our journey through that dark place," Angèle said.

Cumberland nodded and focused his attention on the cooked bird. Mary, who had fetched him a cup of water, returned and sat down next to the boy. She put her hand on his shoulder to comfort him through what was yet to come.

"We met Cumberland on Mr. Brown's steamboat, along with George and Amanthus, the boy's parents. They had been with Junior since Memphis," Angèle began. "They waited for us through the night on Mr. Brown's orders. He hid them away in a stowaway compartment of the ship in case anyone from Cairo boarded while he was attending to our group's predicament. We were almost to Indiana before they came out to meet us. We didn't talk much that first day on the river, just kept our eyes focused on either bank. Waiting. That night, though, we all shared a celebratory dinner as we straddled the dividing line between the free states to our left and the slave states to our right: an *aperitif* before our emancipation. We all told harrowing stories of survival. Some of those tales you have heard this night."

"My father was President Andrew Jackson's personal servant at The Hermitage," Cumberland chimed in, a temporary air of pride in his voice that Patrick found odd. "My mother and I lived on another plantation outside Nashville, near The Hermitage. When our owner moved to Memphis, I wasn't sure if I'd ever see my father again. But after President Jackson died two years ago, the Jacksons hired my father out to the President's nephew, Andrew Donelson, a local politician in Memphis, so that he could be nearer to my mother and me. We certainly appreciated the kindness of that act, but even though we were in the same city, we still didn't live as a family. So, when the opportunity arose to catch a ride on Mr. Brown's steamboat, we three jumped at it without even a final destination in mind. I guess we had our sights set on fleeing into Canadian obscurity."

Patrick, relieved to hear a heartwarming story, asked, "How did you end up here, then? Without them?" As he asked Cumberland those questions, he remembered what Mary had said earlier, "We lost people in those woods, too."

Patrick looked at Angèle, "What happened?"

"The pukwudgie," she said.

* * *

"We made it through the Erie Canal and onto Lake Ontario, where Mr. Brown transferred us into the custody of his brother, Owen, at a port town named Oswego. Owen, Mr. Brown told us, was running firearms between Montreal and Syracuse, and he was going to take us to North Elba near Lake Placid in Essex County to meet a man named Garrit Smith. Smith, it seems, was offering land grants to fugitive slaves, which provided them with the property ownership black folk needed to vote in New York State. The deal sounded pretty good to George and Amanthus, so the sisters and I agreed to travel with them on our way to Nova Scotia."

"I caught passage on a small rabaska from Quebec City to Montreal with a man named Owen Brown!" Patrick said, excited by the intersection of their stories.

"Probably one and the same," Angèle said.

"So, he brought you all the way into the heart of the

Adirondacks?" Patrick said.

"He did. Though, when we arrived in North Elba, it was clear that the bigotry of the white landowners even that far north would cause Garrit Smith's noble experiment to fail. George and Amanthus, thinking of Cumberland more than themselves, decided it would be best to continue on with us through the New York wilderness toward Nova Scotia. Owen Brown left us there but asked that we take a young girl, about the same age as Cumberland, who went by the name of Hany Blackman along with us, as she had no family of her own in the area and Mr. Smith had plans to travel to Washington D.C. with his friend William Chaplin. We agreed and set off on foot due east.

"We had been walking for the better part of a day through the Sentinel Range when we descended into a gorge and darkness. Even though the sun was still well above the horizon, very little light reached its way down to the river that had cut that deep chasm. It was cold, and George suggested that we make camp in the ravine as it would surely be midnight by the time we crawled our way out on the other side. He motioned to a crevice in the steep rock wall and, upon investigation, we found that it opened up into a small cave that would act as a natural shelter. George ushered his family and the rest of us inside.

"The cave was cramped, but not uncomfortable. We dropped our gear and made use of the fading light to refill our water rations and to hunt for food. I started the fire while George and Cumberland attempted to catch fish in the river. They would return empty-handed, but Mary and Emily had managed to forage some dandelion greens that, while bitter, were edible nonetheless. Amanthus won the day, however, when she reappeared from a short hike among the rocks carrying a snapping turtle in both arms.

"How did you manage that? I asked.

""They move slow; kilt it with a stick," she said as she sat down to begin wrapping it in long strands of slick hydrill that she yanked free from the river. Some of the wet vines were ten feet in length, giving us a sense of the water's depth. In the morning, we would have to follow the current in search of a ford where the crossing would be less dangerous.

"When Amanthus finished her preparations, she tossed the celadon shell into the fire, steaming the meat inside. We were all exhausted, so most of us simply slunk down on the ground near the fire to watch the flames light the darkness. Once the meat began to cook, however, we backed away from the reek of old, stagnant mud that filled the air around us. Amanthus said that without a proper washing method and seasoning, the turtle wasn't going to be very appetizing, but it would do the job of filling our bellies and our energy stores for the next day's walk. Of course, we all ate our fill anyhow—unsure, as we were, of what might constitute our next meal whenever it might come. Owen Brown did leave us with a few bars of chocolate that we used to mask the taste of the turtle. For that, we were most thankful.

"As the stars began to punctuate the night sky, we, one-by-one, filed into the slit in the rock face that opened into our secure shelter. It would protect us from the elements and the wildlife. George said that he would take the first watch, which would mostly amount to stoking the fire's ruby glare at the cave's entrance. We didn't have any weapons that might otherwise ward off a bear or coyote or other unnamable marauding creatures, so it was imperative that the fire remain lit. Absalom and Thomas stood their ground on either side of the entrance in mute protest, and remained there as George assured us that he would wake them to take the second watch when he was ready to turn in. We would all need sleep if we were going to make it as far east as the Hudson Valley the next day. "Plus," he added as an afterthought, "I just can't trust anyone else to keep my family safe. Not yet." We all understood, being as we had similarly suffered abuse to one degree or another. Of course, George didn't think of it that way. He figured that his family had been wronged and wasn't no one else going to understand. We never got around to telling George our story. Not sure he'd have believed it even if we had. Once you've been hurt bad enough, it's difficult to place your trust in anyone—especially folks trying to be your friends."

Patrick offered Angèle a smile. The creases at the corners of his eyes were deep with sincerity and sadness. He smoothed his beard as he pondered what she was up to with a statement like that one. There was no comparison, he knew, between what her group had braved and what he had been through in Ireland or aboard the *Agnes*, and he appreciated that she recognized his suffering alongside the atrocities through which she and the others had lived, even if they didn't measure up.

"But," she continued.

Patrick's hand fell from his face, and his smile drooped into a frown. Cumberland's parents did not arrive with him at the lighthouse. Nor did Hany Blackman. Mary had said that they lost people in the woods. Patrick feared that he was about to learn whether that meant the two groups were separated, or that three of their companions would never again walk from among the trees.

"We were not the only ones in those woods set on easing our hunger pains that evening. The stench of that cooked snapper invited unexpected, and unwanted, attention to our camp," Angèle said.

"The pukwudgie," Patrick said.

"So it seems," Angèle said. "We all slept eerily sound that night. When the light of the day finally burst through the fissure, flooding the small cave with sunbeams, the lot of us simultaneously stirred, like heliotropes, as if waking from a spell. I knew instantly that something was wrong. Absalom and Thomas were still inside the cave, where George should have been asleep following his shift tending to the fire. I scrambled to get outside first in case I could protect Amanthus and

Cumberland from some grisly sight, but they both beat me to the opening. Their screams stopped me cold. When I recovered from the shock, I exited the cave to find George's wife and son trying to move a boulder the size of a horse carriage from atop his body.

"The others filed from the cave and offered their help pushing the rock, but it would not budge. We agreed that George must have taken shelter beneath the boulder and fallen asleep. At some point during the night, the massive rock worked free from its perch atop a few smaller stones and crushed him. In hindsight, we should have suspected something far more sinister. Only George's lower half was pinned beneath the rock, which meant there should have been an audible scream or a cry for help. Instead, we found his skull staring up at us in a grimace of pain. His bones had been picked clean of all skin, meat, and organs. Something had trapped and eaten him."

"You think it was the pukwudgie?" Patrick asked.

"I suppose it could have been a small horde, but I haven't ever heard of them doing anything as heinous as that. According to Abenaki folklore, they have certainly lured people to their deaths using magic, and have been known to kidnap children or push them off cliffs, but to eat them—"

"It was the creature, then. The red-eyed devil," Patrick said.

"It seems likely," Angèle said.

"But what could eat the flesh clean off a man like that?" Patrick said. "The Beast of Gévaudan?"

"Something far more threatening. Though I believed it to exist only in the northwest territories of Canada, near the Yukon," Angèle said.

"Well? What is it?" Patrick prodded.

"A demon," Angèle said.

Patrick recalled instantly the letter he had found in the roll top desk and nearly knocked his chair over he stood up so fast to retrieve it. The others watched him, wondering what he was after. There were only two books on the desk, a diary and a Bible. He picked up the Bible and offered it to Angèle.

"What's this?" she asked.

"Open it," Patrick said.

"And what am I looking for?" she wondered.

"There's a letter tucked behind the front cover that may mean something to you that it didn't mean to me," he said.

Angèle opened the book and unfolded the letter, which she read aloud to the group. "Caleb." She stopped to look at Patrick. "Who's Caleb?"

"From what I gather, he may have been the original keeper of this lighthouse," Patrick said.

Angèle nodded and continued reading aloud, "During our travels throughout the Onondaga territory, we have discovered a salt spring located at the southern end of Lake Gannentaha. It was there we had hoped to establish a site for the French mission. We tested the water of the spring, which the Indians are afraid to drink, saying that it is inhabited by a demon, who makes it foul." Angèle paused to consider this new information.

"Interesting, yes?" Patrick said.

"Indeed. I'm beginning to fear that what I assumed may be true," Angèle said. Then she continued with the rest of the letter, "I found the fountain of salt water, from which we evaporated a little salt as natural as that from the sea, some of which we shall carry to Quebec. I have included among the enclosed supplies from the Plymouth Trading Company a small parcel of the Onondaga salt that Aoife might use for preserving your garden vegetables through the winter months. Blessings to the children. Signed, Fr. Simon Le Moyne."

"So?" Patrick said. "You have a theory?"

Before she could answer, Cumberland spoke: "I've heard that name before."

"What?" Angèle asked.

"Aoife. When I was upstairs. I dreamed of a fair-skinned

woman with long hair that blazed the color of the Charleston Trinity Church fire. She lay beside me on the bed and sang the most beautiful lullabies in a language I could not understand. She kissed me, and told me her name was Aoife."

Patrick's face drained of all its color, and his jaw hung slack with bewilderment. "I've had that dream as well."

"What do you mean you've had that dream, as well?" Angèle asked, perturbed.

"I mean that exactly those things Cumberland claims to have experienced earlier today happened to me as well, the very first night I slept in the bed upstairs. It didn't strike me as all that strange then because there is a painting of the woman and her family hanging opposite the bed. I figured my imagination just—"

Angèle dropped the note and leaped up from the table. She darted up the stairs two-at-a-time to see for herself the painting of this woman who, she suspected, had not only golden-red hair but also melancholy, emerald eyes.

The others ran up the stone steps after her. When they arrived, out of breath, they saw Angèle standing before the painting as if mesmerized. Without taking her eyes from the portrait, she said to Cumberland and Patrick, "It wasn't a dream you two shared."

They looked at one another, confused by Angèle's declaration.

Her lips twisted into a smile. She had finally pieced together the identity of the specter she saw haunting the lantern gallery upon exiting the woods—a specter who, Angèle now knew, based upon Le Moyne's letter, had been in residence at the lighthouse for at least 200 years. Time enough to learn what hunted in the forest. "I had mistaken her for Baron Samedi's wife, Maman Brigitte. That is why I thought the lighthouse would be safe."

"What do you mean—you've seen her before?" Patrick asked.

"Of course. This is Aoife's home."

* * *

"Why is she still here?" Patrick asked, his skin crawling at the thought that he had been living with a ghost for months.

"That I do not know," Angèle said. "But worry not, we shall ask her."

"Is she not dangerous?" Patrick asked.

"Do you have reason to believe she would harm us?" Angèle countered. "You didn't even know she was here until a few minutes ago."

Patrick assented the point.

"Should I get Papa's things?" Mary asked.

"That won't be necessary. Aoife is not in Guinee, she lives inside the lighthouse," Angèle said. "And that bodes well for us."

"I don't follow," Cumberland said.

"The Baron has a fondness for mortal women, especially their trapped spirits. Perhaps he could be persuaded to cross over into our world for the opportunity to..." She paused. "...meet Aoife."

"And?" Patrick said.

"And, we are going to need the Baron's help," Angèle said.

"Why? What do you think stalks those woods, Angèle? Certainly nothing so threatening as to require the Baron." Emily said.

"A Wendigo," Angèle said sharply. "I had my suspicions when," she looked to Cumberland. "Well, never you mind. According to Algonquian folklore, Wendigoag were once human beings who—for whatever reason—resorted to cannibalism. Once a person consumes the flesh of a human, the Algonquian believe they are transformed into an insatiable creature of gaunt physique. Their rate of growth keeps pace with the flesh they eat; thus, they remain ever-hungry giants. I've never seen one, but supposedly their yellowed fangs and long tongues resemble those of a wolf and their stretched skin gives off the eerie smell of decomposition. As you have witnessed, Patrick, their garnet-colored eyes are said to glow like gemstones in the darkness."

"But you said it was a demon, something otherworldly," Patrick protested.

"To be sure. Another Indian nation, the Onondaga, believe that an evil spirit possesses the man, inflicting upon him some sort of cannibalistic psychosis. If this is true, and the Jesuit priest disturbed a demon in the Gannentaha Salt Spring, then it may be that Caleb was possessed by the evil lurking in the salt that was sent to him as a gift."

"How can we be sure?" Patrick asked.

"I will try to speak with Aoife, but in the meantime, have you uncovered anything else that might provide us with more information?" Angèle asked.

"There is a book of paintings—"

"Bring it to me!" Angèle demanded. Patrick left the room to retrieve the watercolor diary from the desk on the first floor, and Angèle climbed the ladder toward the lantern gallery, leaving Cumberland, Mary, and Emily alone in the bedchamber. The sisters began preparing an altar in the event Angèle decided to summon the Baron. They took a purple pillowcase from one of the decorative pillows and tore it down the center so that it would run the length of the dresser. Mary set out a series of white candles and prepared Angèle's chalk for the drawing of the Baron's vèvè. Cumberland added two bottles of rum and asked Emily if she thought he should ask Absalom and Thomas to bring up the trunk.

"Let's wait and see," Emily answered.

"Wait and see what?" Patrick asked, entering the room from the dark stairwell.

"Angèle went up to the gallery," Emily said, eluding his question.

Patrick started toward the ladder to deliver the book but stopped before he reached the first rung. "Do you think she's right?" he asked the group. "A wendigo?"

"I've never known her to be wrong," Mary said.

"And what if she is right?" Cumberland asked. "Then what do we do?"

No one answered, nor could they. Patrick took the silence as an invitation to leave but balked before he continued to climb. "Cumberland. What happened to your mother?"

"I don't know," he admitted. "They won't tell me."

Patrick looked at the sisters, "How can you keep his own mother's fate a secret?"

"It's too horrid," Emily said.

Mary shivered as if to throw off the memory of it all.

"I'm okay not knowing. I saw what those beasts did to my father. I don't need the details," Cumberland said. "I was with Hany when it happened—whatever it was."

"There's another mystery. Where is Hany Blackman?" Patrick said. "Angèle speaks of trust, but I don't know half of what happened to you all in the forest!"

Cumberland looked at Emily as if for permission. She gave it to him with a curt nod of her head.

"After my father died, I set out to find some wood to construct a cross to mark his grave, which my mother was digging with the help of the sisters," Cumberland said.

"Gravedigging is somber work, even if it is only to put a stranger to rest," Mary said.

"I know," Patrick said. "Though it's not as awful as disturbing them."

"What do you mean by that?" Emily asked.

"Nothing," Patrick said.

"I borrowed the hatchet that Mr. Brown had given us in our supply bundle and set out to chop down a tree that would provide me with the length of wood necessary to fashion a cross to mark my father's tomb. Hany insisted that she come along to keep me company. We probably walked a mile or two, following the river downstream until we reached a point where the current rushed so furiously that we almost couldn't hear one another speak. It was then that Hany pointed to a misshapen tree that bent at an unnatural, ninety-degree angle as if someone had warped it into a direction marker."

"You cut that tree," Patrick said gravely.

"I did," Cumberland said, thinking nothing of Patrick's tone. "I split the horizontal trunk in two so that Hany and I could each carry a section back to camp. We walked only a few hundred feet before she noticed a sleek black horse with a flowing mane and luminescent golden eyes grazing on the bank of the churning river. Hany quickly made a set of reigns out of swallow-wort vines and fashioned a bit from a piece of white pine bark. She told me that she had been a stable maid on a South Carolina cotton plantation before escaping to a small Huguenot town called New Paltz by way of the Delaware and Hudson Rivers. It turned out that they weren't exactly abolitionists, so she immediately left for North Elba.

"Hany figured to tame the stallion and use it to carry our supplies. And she did." Cumberland fell silent. He closed his eyes and watched his memory of the horse bowing down to let Hany ascend. He continued, "The horse gave her no fight. In fact, it invited her to climb upon its back. Sitting atop the beast, Hany smiled down at me and said, "It must be domesticated. Maybe there's a farm nearby?" Then it reared up and bolted headlong into the river and dove beneath the current. Neither of them reappeared."

"Drown'd by the Kelpie's wrath, no doubt,"[8] Patrick said.

"I don't know what a kelpie is, but I'm sure it was one of those same faeries that killed my father, only this time shapeshifted into a horse, keen on drowning and devouring Hany Blackman."

"I'd say you know exactly what a kelpie is, Cumberland. **Púca by a different name.**"

"Well, I used the remaining swallow-wort vines to tether the cross and planted it in the ground at the river's edge in memory of Hany. I figured my father already had a gravestone, anyhow."

"I suppose that's true," Patrick agreed.

"When I returned to the camp my mother was gone."

Patrick wasn't sure what to say but wanted to offer the boy his sympathy. "Maybe it's better this way," he stumbled. "I don't mean it's better that your parents are gone, but only that you didn't exactly have to see it." He recalled the overwhelming sadness of watching his parents starve to death in the Ennistymon Union Workhouse despite his best efforts to save them.

Cumberland said nothing.

"Here," Patrick said and handed the book of watercolors to Cumberland. "Take this up to Angèle. See if she can make any sense of it."

Cumberland took the diary from Patrick and shoved it into his pocket and began ascending the ladder. Before he disappeared through the hatch into the watch room, he looked down at Mary and Emily knowingly. "It's okay if you tell him," he said. "We're all in this together now."

When his feet vanished, and the hatch closed, Patrick asked, "Was it the faeries that took his mother?"

"I don't think so," Emily said. "Though I suppose it could have been."

"It was snakes," Mary blurted. "Thousands of 'em."

Emily confirmed her sister's statement. "We were digging George's grave when the ground gave way. A sinkhole opened up beneath our feet. Mary was nearest the edge and managed to pull me back from the widening pit. We both scrambled to the safety of the rocks. From there we watched, helpless, as the ground swallowed Amanthus."

"It all happened so fast," Mary said, "from the first shift of the soil to the settling of the dust. Emily and I climbed down as soon as it was safe to see if we might be able to clear away some of the rubble to pull her free, but when we looked into the hole we saw only Amanthus's terrified face for a split second before it sank beneath—"

"Snakes," Emily said.

Patrick gasped and raised a hand to cover his mouth.

"Magic or not, we were digging on top of a snake den. When the ground got too thin, it gave away unearthing thousands of hibernating snakes. The shift disturbed them, and their thrashing bodies pulled Amanthus deep into the pit like quicksand."

Patrick imagined that the torrent of serpents was not unlike the deadly chop of an angry ocean. The vision brought to mind his dream of Rory's body disappearing beneath the Atlantic swells.

"Without knowing the whole story, Cumberland was right, Amanthus was just...gone." As Emily concluded her tale, something in the watch room above them emitted a low, dragging wail that surged into an excruciating, unholy scream.

# Part III

# The Wendigo

# Chapter 9

# Ruin

Patrick and the sisters clutched at their ears. At first, they had thought Angèle and Cumberland had opened the lantern gallery windows letting in an icy moan from the wintery blackness outside. It grew colder in the bedchamber, even though the watch room hatch was shut tight and the heavy curtains remained drawn across the small window. The assailing scream intensified, paralyzing the three with fear and pain. The window and mirror both shattered, spraying shards of jagged glass across the room. And then it was over.

They watched with incredulity as the veneer of simple comfort was stripped from the interior of the lighthouse. As if the otherworldly bellow had exposed some supernatural façade, the once homey lighthouse now appeared to them in ruin. Patrick, Mary, and Emily studied their new surroundings: the stone walls were black with mold, the bedsheets upon which they sat were sun-faded and threadbare, the very floor sagged with the weight of centuries.

The three waited in the still silence for the screams to begin anew. They heard nothing, except for a deafening ringing in their ears. After a few minutes, Patrick motioned that he was going to inspect the hatch and that the sisters should remain in the uncanny bedchamber. Mary and Emily both shot Patrick panicked looks that wordlessly pleaded for him not to leave, but he had already crossed the room and was placing a boot on the first rung of the ladder. It immediately snapped under his weight. Patrick reached out to grab another rung to stop himself from toppling backward but managed only to pluck it free from the rusted side rails. He crashed to the floor, scattering a cloud of dust into the air. "Help me push the bed over to the opening," he said as he coughed.

They lined themselves across one side of the massive bed and leaned their hips into the wooden frame, pushing until it was directly under the hatch. Patrick then upended the empty bassinet and stacked it atop the bed. The sisters offered steadying hands as he climbed the unstable pile. Patrick balanced himself atop the bassinet while he worked to free the lever that held the hatch in place. It gave way with a squeal, and Patrick hoisted himself through the hole into the unsettling darkness above.

The air was stale and hard to breathe. It reminded Patrick of the mildewed crypts he had plundered with the Priest in the West of Ireland. He choked on dust and clawed cobwebs from his face. It was not the watch room that he had traversed countless times on his way to the lantern gallery. And, yet, it was the same. Cracks in the masonry, slimy with mildew, had admitted more than weather. The room crawled with spiders that had spun the isolated area into a colony of nests. Patrick suffered a minor attack of vertigo as the walls, thick with creeping bugs, appeared in constant motion. He paused only long enough to retch upon the floor, which gave the spiders time to scurry up his boots and into his pant legs, down his neck and into the open collar of his shirt. Patrick kicked and swatted to no avail, so he darted for the small set of crumbling stairs that would lead him into the night air of the open gallery above. Once out of the windowless watch room and into the moonlit gallery, Patrick began furiously shaking the spiders from his body. Those that he didn't smash between clothes and skin scurried back into the darkness from whence they had come. "We're going to need fire," Patrick said, flicking a few remaining pests to the floor, "for the spiders, and the cold."

Angèle sat upon a barrel of paraffin oil. Cumberland stood next to her, blood dripping from his ears. Neither of them turned to look at Patrick. They fixed their stares upon the translucent figure of Aoife hovering before them. Patrick would have described her as looking relieved had he focused on her long enough to assess the ghost's features. As it were, his eyes peered straight through her shimmering form to spy on the lake below a series of faint navigation lights. Where he hadn't seen a single ship during his six-month residency, he now saw two merchant vessels traveling single-file behind an icebreaker that propelled its reinforced bow into the frozen surface of Lake Champlain. Patrick's mouth hung open with restored hope.

"Aoife has lifted the veil," Angèle said. "She has allowed us to see beyond the curse."

"Kate's curse?" Patrick asked, still confused by the sudden changes to the lighthouse and its environs.

"That may be only a single thread weaved into a more complex web of enchantment," Angèle said.

"That scream," Patrick said.

"I figured you would have recognized the *ban síde*," Angèle said.

"Banshee!" Patrick said, turning his attention to Aoife's ghost. "Her shriek heralds death. You are lamenting someone?" he asked.

Aoife lowered her eyes and bowed her head.

"One of us," Cumberland said.

"That I cannot tell you," Aoife whispered, forlorn.

Patrick's eyes widened at the sound of her voice. "You can speak!" he exclaimed, his hope further bolstered by this revelation. "What happened here?" Patrick asked, motioning all around him to the lighthouse.

"Nothing more than you can now see this lighthouse through your own eyes instead of mine," Aoife said.

"I preferred it the other way, thank you," Patrick said. Then more seriously, "You can't mean that I've been living in this wreckage all winter. How did I not freeze to death? How is it that I am not covered in spider bites? That my lungs are not choked with dust?"

"That is the curse. You experienced what you believed to be

true," Aoife explained.

Patrick thought carefully about Aoife's words. Then he asked, "So, if we doubt that ravenous creatures inhabit the woods, then we can walk safely through them?"

"Yes," Aoife replied. "*If* you truly believe that is the case."

"But I was hunted by the pukwudgie when I neither believed nor disbelieved in them," Patrick said. "I had no knowledge of their existence."

"You delivered the púca into those woods; they were born of the song you brought with you aboard the *Agnes*," said Aoife.

"But how did you…" Patrick asked.

"I know of everything that happens in the woods," Aoife said.

"Including what will happen," Angèle interjected.

Aoife nodded.

"Something evil haunts those woods. I suspect a wendigo," Angèle said.

\* \* \*

"Open that book," Aoife instructed, her facial wounds weeping spectral blood that floated toward the floor, but disappeared before reaching her feet.

Angèle peeled back the diary's cover to reveal a military scene in watercolor, above which Aoife had written in script, *11 September 1649: Siege of Drogheda*.

"In January of that year," Aoife began, "King Charles the First of House Stuart was beheaded under a death warrant signed by the rapacious ogre, Oliver Cromwell. He's the one did that to our home." She pointed toward her painting of catapults launching peat naphtha at the burning city walls. In the foreground, Cromwell sat atop his white steed, aiming a pistol at the face of Sir Arthur Aston, who had ridden down the great mound on the south bank of the River Boyne to surrender Millmount Fort. "Cromwell never fired that pistol," Aoife said. "His soldiers dashed Aston's brains out with the Royalist's own wooden leg. Someone had said that Aston used it to conceal gold coins."

"That's awful," Cumberland commented.

"Aye. In the wake of that bloody conquest, Cromwell executed every Catholic implicated in the Rebellion of 1641 that saw the massacre of Protestant settlers in Ulster. Cromwell confiscated our land and deported the rest of us to the West Indies as indentured laborers. Caleb Doyle and I were engaged to be married the following June, but we said our vows at sea as part of a mass ceremony alongside the other couples destined to work the sugar plantations on Barbados. Shortly thereafter, we thought a stroke of luck had been delivered to us when our ship encountered the English Armada's Virginian blockade, and we were forced north along the colonial coastline. The war had stymied English shipping, and any vessel that wasn't diverted to military use was seized, along with their cargos. Had we continued south, we would have been prey to buccaneers, or worse still we would have reached our destination and suffered under the lash."

"Why would pirates be interested in slave ships?" Patrick asked.

"African slaves were worth about 50 sterling per head, so there was money to be made in the slave trade," said Aoife.

Angèle nodded knowingly.

"We Irish brought in no more than 5 sterling apiece, so our lot was used for more carnal pleasures," Aoife continued. "The worst offender at that time was François l'Olonnais. While the storms we faced to the north were wicked in their own right, death by drowning was preferable to the tortures doled out by l'Olonnais and his rogues."

"How did you end up here?" Patrick asked.

"Our Captain elected to divert course to the Massachusetts Bay Colony, considering the authorities there were sympathetic to the Parliamentary cause and had supported the English

Commonwealth, and that the fur and lumber industries had established trading lines between the Machigonne peninsula north of Boston and the West Indies. When tensions off the coast of Virginia eased, the slavers would send us to the sugar plantations along with a shipment of pelts. Before we could safely enter the port, a violent nor'easter smashed our ship against a ledge off Cape Elizabeth. Wreckage and bodies spread across Casco Bay. Caleb and I fortuitously washed ashore on one of the smaller islands that the Abenaki Indians used as a fishing ground. It was they who brought us back to the mainland and delivered us into the care of Fr. Gabriel Druillettes—one of several French Jesuit missionaries laboring among the Abenaki. We stayed with them for a year, until 1653, when Gabriel was called to Cloven Rock to meet a fellow Jesuit, Fr. Simon Le Moyne, in an effort to broker peace negotiations between the Algonquin tribes to the north and the Iroquois people to the south. We helped the Jesuits build this lighthouse as a beacon of hope upon the dividing lines of those two great nations. Simon appointed Caleb, me, and the twins as its inaugural keepers."

"Twins?" Angèle asked.

"Yes. We were blessed with twin boys shortly after the completion of the lighthouse," Aoife said with a hint of sadness in her voice. "Declan and Áedán."

"What happened to them?" Patrick asked.

"Turn the page," Aoife said. She squeezed shut her eyes to quell a tear as Angèle thumbed to the following painting of two red clouds that resembled a condensed fog. From where he stood, behind Angèle's shoulder, Patrick stared into what he recognized as a pair of monochromatic eyes. When Angèle turned around and lifted her gaze to meet Patrick's, he nodded gravely, affirming their danger.

"Again," Aoife commanded. Angèle obeyed.

Cumberland gasped when he saw the creature staring back at him from the page. It was both man and beast. Its hair, black as a raven, hung past its shoulders, though bunches of it had been tied up with strands of rope to resemble antlers; twigs and leaves were tangled in its hair in such a way that it looked as if they grew out from the creature's head. Its face was caked with a thin mask of mud that did little to conceal its desiccated skin. The lips were dry and cracked and oozing pus; they pulled tight against greying teeth. But it was the hungry, pupil-less eyes that caused Cumberland to look away. They had sunk deep into their sockets, which had caused the creature's nose to collapse against its skull to the point that both nostrils flared permanently outward—as if to better catch the scent of potential prey.

"How did you get such a good look at it that you were able to paint this?" Patrick asked.

"It snatched my babies from my arms. As it tore into them, I fled," she said with palpable self-disgust.

"If the wendigo ate Declan and Áedán, then what lies in the graves just inside the woods?" Patrick asked.

"All that was left of them," Aoife said. "Crushed bones."

"But the painting? Your children are grown." Angèle said.

"A dream," Aoife admitted. "I painted that portrait after they were gone to console my grief. It didn't work."

"And the girl?" Angèle asked.

"Never even born," Aoife said.

"I'm so sorry, dear," Angèle said, reaching out a hand to console the ghost as if she were a living being in need of physical comfort.

"That thing," Patrick cut in, "is that—"

"Caleb." Aoife finished.

Patrick studied the watercolor painting for any sign of likeness to the portrait hanging in the bedchamber. He could find none.

"I know now that it wasn't really Caleb ate our boys, that some dark spirit possessed him, but I couldn't forgive myself for not protecting any of them from that evil. I knew it would come back, that their small bodies would not be enough to satiate its appetite. So, to prevent the wendigo from harming our unborn daughter, I tossed myself from atop the cliff into the freezing waters of the lake below. We are still down there beneath the waves, she and I. It cannot get to us there."

"Your daughter's spirit was able to move on to Guinee, then? And you were not," Angèle said.

"Grainne is with her brothers in Heaven," Aoife said.

Patrick rolled his eyes. Anger shadowed Angèle's face at his continued skepticism.

Taking no notice, Aoife continued, "I chose to stay, to watch over our home, and to welcome Caleb into the afterlife once the spirit is finished with him."

"We need to get out of here," Patrick said. "Is there a safe way through the woods?"

"No, the wendigo will find you. Or the pukwudgie will lure you to it," Aoife said.

This, Patrick believed.

"Cumberland," Angèle said.

"Yes, Ma'am?"

"Run ahead and tell Absalom and Thomas to fetch my trunk and deliver it to that small cemetery in the woods," Angèle instructed.

"Are we going in there again?" Cumberland fretted.

"We are. But this time we're inviting the Baron."

* * *

When they reached the ground floor of the lighthouse, Patrick and Angèle were met by the sullen face of Cumberland. "They're gone," was all he said.

"Who's gone?" Patrick asked.

"Everyone," said Cumberland.

"Where did they go?" Angèle asked.

"I'm not sure, Ma'am. I came down through that hellish

watch room into the bedchamber and found it empty, as I did each room after that."

"Where would Mary and Emily have gotten off to?" Angèle wondered.

"The door was still bolted shut from the inside, so it's not possible that they left the lighthouse," Cumberland said. "Nor is it possible that Absalom and Thomas, who are also missing, came in."

"That door does tend to open of its own volition," Patrick offered.

"I opened that door for you," Aoife said when she appeared from above.

"Okay, you've claimed to know everything that goes on in your woods; where are they?" Patrick demanded.

"The women are not in the forest, and are therefore safe," Aoife said. "The eunuchs on the other hand—"

"Was your keening meant for them, then?" Patrick asked.

"My lament was not intended for any one of you in particular. I mourn you all," Aoife said.

"We're all going to die!" Cumberland worried aloud.

"Do you know what happened to Absalom and Thomas?" Angèle pressed.

"Yes. The pukwudgie have taken them, and your magic will not bring them back this time," warned Aoife.

"Those creatures can leave the woods?" Patrick asked.

"No, but they are masterful at getting others to enter against their will. Somehow, they enticed your giants," Aoife said.

"Impossible," Angèle breathed.

"And, yet, they are gone," Aoife said.

"Cumberland, you and I will carry the trunk. Whatever you're hiding inside had better get us out of this wretched place," Patrick said to Angèle.

Cumberland looked at her for permission. Angèle waved her hand for them to be gone. Absalom and Thomas had placed the trunk just inside the entryway, which is where it remained for Patrick and Cumberland to lift. They each summoned all of their strength to hoist it mere inches from the ground. "What is in this thing?" Patrick puffed as he and Cumberland shuffled their feet in unison through the doorway and into the snowy night.

"Damballa," Angèle finally revealed, and Cumberland dropped his end to the ground and backed away. The force with which the trunk crashed into the frozen earth yanked Patrick forward, and he fell across the top. Seeing Cumberland's reaction to the word *Damballa*, Patrick, too, scrambled away from the trunk.

"What is a Damballa?" he asked.

"The Serpent Father," Cumberland responded not taking his eyes from the trunk. "Creator of all life."

"You mean God?" Patrick asked.

"Don't be silly," Angèle chastised. "God is not in that wooden box. Damballa is my mother's snake."

"Why do you have your mother's snake in that trunk?" Patrick asked.

"You will see," Angèle said. "Now, take it to the cemetery."

"I'm pretty sure your snake is going to die in the cold," Patrick said.

"I will keep her warm," said Angèle.

Patrick and Cumberland regained their composure and limped the heavy trunk toward the woods—more carefully now that they knew there was something living inside. Angèle followed the pair into the night's darkness but turned when she felt Aoife was no longer behind her. "Are you not coming with us?" she asked.

"I am not permitted to leave the lighthouse but for one reason," Aoife informed her.

"And who is responsible for your incarceration?"

"I don't know."

"We shall bring the Baron to you, then." Angèle turned and

walked toward the woods into which Patrick and Cumberland had already disappeared with the trunk. Aoife watched from the open doorway of the ruined lighthouse.

* * *

Beneath the pale light of the yellow moon, Patrick dug his spade into the frozen graves of Aoife's twin sons and retrieved their brittle skulls for the Baron's macabre altar. "I had hoped that I wouldn't ever have to do this sort of work again," Patrick wheezed.

"Again?" Cumberland asked as he prepared the last of their spiced rum and the sole remaining cigar for the Baron's arrival.

Patrick did not elaborate but crawled from the shallow hole with a mutilated skull in each hand. He rubbed them gently across his chest to remove the clay that had lodged inside the cavities. The freed dirt left a chilling imprint on his shirt that looked like two moaning ghouls.

Meanwhile, Angèle had changed her dress and now appeared wearing a white linen djellaba and a haint blue turban wrapped around her head. Draped around her neck were heavy strands of purple and black Orisha beads. Upon her shoulders rested Damballa, an eight-foot-long albino African Rock Python. It swayed with her as she sang to Papa Legba.

"Legba nan baye-a
Legba nan baye-a
Legba nan baye-a
Se ou ki pote drapo
Se ou k ap pare soley pou lwa yo."

Angèle could feel the snake contracting its muscles in quick spasms as if shivering to keep warm. Patrick watched with worry as Damballa coiled himself ever tighter around Angèle's upper torso to collect her body heat. Finally the snake's head hovered next to Angèle's ear, flicking its forked tongue as if whispering to her some dark secret. Angèle acknowledged Damballa's message with a slight bow of her head. She then shouted into the wooded darkness, "Lord of the Cemetery! Patriarch of the Guédé! Come, drink with us!"

Patrick jumped, startled by the ferocious power of her voice. He quickly shifted his attention to Cumberland and waited to see if the Baron would possess the boy. Nothing happened.

"Baron Samedi! Spirit of the last night! We invite you into these cursed woods to smoke with us!" Angèle yelled louder, seemingly unconcerned that the noise might attract the attention of the wendigo. When still the Baron did not appear, she uncoiled Damballa from around her body and used the snake's nose to draw the Baron's *vèvè* in the snow atop Caleb's empty gravesite—a memorial Aoife had prepared for her lost husband. "My mother, Marie Laveau, Voodoo Queen of New Orleans, requests your company." At the mention of her mother's name, the ground beneath Angèle's feet began to swell as if something were pushing up out of the tomb. At first, a hand appeared. Then another. Finally, the Baron heaved himself free from the ground, tipped his black top hat to Cumberland, and winked at Angèle.

"Where is your mother," he said, straightening his black suitcoat and brushing debris from his scarlet vest with a gloved hand.

Angèle draped Damballa around his neck, and the snake spoke, "Baron of the Boneyard, welcome."

Baron Samedi threw back his skull and brayed a deep laughter into the night sky. "Marie!" he said heartily and stroked the snake's head.

"What is going on," Patrick asked anyone who would respond.

"Mr. Gallagher," said the Baron, "you seem confused. Let's have a drink, shall we?" He picked up two glasses of rum from the makeshift altar and handed one to Patrick. He held the other out for Patrick to salute, and once the glass rims had clanked together, both men swallowed their rum. "Don't be shy," the Baron said to Angèle and Cumberland. "Drink with us!" The two did as they were told and drank the remaining glasses of rum. "You need something I presume," said the Baron, watching Angèle lick rum from her lips. He loosened a brown jug that hung from his side and refilled everyone's glass with a portion of rum from his private stock.

"Information," Angèle said flirtatiously, playing into the Baron's temptations.

"Why does he think the snake is your mother?" Patrick asked as the Baron stooped slowly to pick up the lonely cigar that lay on the altar at Angèle's feet. He righted himself before her, and slipped the cigar between his lips, smiling a satisfied grin that revealed his inky teeth.

"The snake is my mother," Angèle said without further explanation. She did not take her eyes from the Baron, who had placed his hands on her hips, drawing her ever closer to him.

"I am here for Marie," the Baron said to Angèle. "I will give you what you need."

"What is going on?" Patrick hissed to Cumberland.

"I think Miss. Marie has possessed the snake," Cumberland offered.

"Bi-location! The boy is correct! Do you remember what Papa Legba told you?" asked the Baron.

"Yes, sir," Cumberland said. He stared into the snow as he was unable to meet the lwa's wild stare.

"What did he tell you?" Patrick asked.

Cumberland didn't respond to Patrick. He shrank from the scene into the shadows of the trees, his fear of the woods replaced by humiliation or remorse, Patrick could not say.

"What can you tell us of the wendigo?" Angèle asked the Baron.

He slid his skeletal hands across her backside and squeezed her flesh. "Everything," he whispered slowly. "For a price."

"What do you want?" Patrick inquired, knowing all-too-well the answer.

"I said that I would give you what you need, after you give me what I *need*," said the Baron.

"I have something for you," Angèle said devilishly.

"Good," the Baron replied. He kissed the snake and said, "Marie, we are even." He handed Damballa back to Angèle, who slid the snake back into the trunk atop a mound of silver coins. She then hooked the Baron's arm and led him toward the lighthouse.

"Alright, Cumberland. Let's haul this thing back inside," said Patrick, watching the glow of the Baron's cigar fade into the distance. "Cumberland? Cumberland!" He performed a hurried search around the gravesite where he had seen the boy wander into the woods and was about to run back toward the lighthouse to warn Angèle when Cumberland reappeared. "Damn it, Cumberland, you gave me a scare!" Patrick said.

"I'm sorry. I just didn't want to be around the Baron if it wasn't completely necessary," said Cumberland.

"Understandable," Patrick said. "Here, grab the other side of the trunk and let's get back inside before the faeries show up."

"Or worse," Cumberland added.

* * *

Aoife watched from above as Angèle and Baron Samedi approached her lighthouse. Though she could not hear what they said, she knew that they were discussing her future at Cloven Rock. Aoife considered barring the doors and retreating into her illusion, but she knew that the Baron would effortlessly pierce her protective veil. Storm clouds had moved in from the northeast, blocking out the winter sun. Heavy snowflakes began to fall to the ground, covering the tracks between the lighthouse and the woods. Soon the lighthouse would once again appear abandoned. The charming scene reminded her of the day she had decided to end her life and that of her unborn daughter to save them both from the torment of Caleb's bite. Their fall from the cliff was almost graceful: the green velvet dress fluttered about them in an ethereal dance until Aoife's face crashed into a protruding rock. As her body slowly sank into the abyss, the velvet dress curled into a bloom around her, like the slow emergence of a lily flower from its bud. Aoife died instantly, but Grainne survived the initial impact. She lived in her dead mother's effete womb until all of the oxygenated blood had been depleted. Aoife's spirit hugged at her sinking corporeal body and sang to Grainne as she slowly suffocated in utero.

Seoithín, seo hó, mo stór é, mo leanbh
Mo sheoid gan cealg, mo chuid gan tsaoil mhór
Seothín seo ho, nach mór é an taitneamh
Mo stóirín na leaba, na chodladh gan brón.
A leanbh mo chléibh go n-eirí do chodhladh leat
Séan is sonas gach oíche do chóir
Tá mise le do thaobh ag guídhe ort na mbeannacht
Seothín a leanbh is codail go foill.

In the murky depths of Lake Champlain, Grainne suffocated. Guédé Nibo accompanied her spirit through the gates of Guinee unseen by Aoife. She had said her goodbyes during their descent, knowing well that she would not be granted the chance to apologize to Grainne's spirit. Aoife's God had condemned her to relive the suicidal plunge each night as penance.

When Angèle arrived with the Baron, Aoife was eager to accept his invitation as that would end her misery. "Your husband is gone forever, dear girl," the Baron said in an attempt to get her to accompany him into the spirit world. "The demon left Caleb's body as soon as it successfully enticed him to devour the flesh of your twins. It was that savage act of consumption that transformed him into the immortal beast that roams the forest in want of meat."

"Then there is nothing left here for me," Aoife anxiously agreed.

"Accompany me to Guinee, then, where you may join the family Guédé," the Baron offered.

"You're going to pimp her for information?" Patrick accused Angèle, who was shocked into silence for she hadn't thought of it in quite the same way.

"Patrick, your tone offends me. I am rescuing dear Aoife from an eternal prison of heartbreak and longing. With me, she will be the governess of Marassa Jumeaux, the divine twins, and honored as a lwa of fertility."

"This is not your choice, Patrick," said Aoife. "It is mine alone. And while I do not deserve this opportunity, I will accept it."

Patrick sneered at what he perceived as Baron Samedi's unstated lewd intent. "So that's it, then? You're going to take away the spirit protecting this lighthouse—and us? Are we to fend for ourselves against this curse?"

"Not entirely, I will tell you how to solve your wendigo problem," said the Baron. "The beast will never die of natural causes—though its hunger is insatiable, it cannot be starved. Though you may wound it with an ordinary weapon, you cannot kill it with such as it will regenerate. You must either burn a wendigo and scatter its ashes in the winds, or stake its heart with silver."

"Not so unlike The Beast of Gévaudan after all," Patrick said to Angèle, who looked at him confused. "Jean Chastel shot the beast with a silver bullet in 1676, ending its three-year reign of terror across Southern France," he explained.

"Three years!" the Baron spat. "Your wendigo is two centuries old! It is a supernatural hunter that will detect your elevated heartbeat from miles away and smell you from further yet. And it can mimic human voices to confuse and disorient you in its enchanted woods. Worse still—"

"Worse?" Cumberland said.

"—It is virtually invisible as it moves thrice as fast as you can even imagine and it can't be seen from the flank."

"I've seen it," Patrick said.

"Because it wanted to be seen!" the Baron countered. "That is part of the hunt. Your fear works in its favor." He took a satisfied draw from his cigar to celebrate the impact of his point. When he released the smoke into the air, it took the form of the wendigo's growling face. The Baron pierced the smoke cloud with the silver tip of his walking stick, dispersing the creature's likeness. "My advice: find some silver."

"Patrick, stoke the fire. Cumberland, empty the coins from my trunk into that cauldron. We'll melt them down and plate the fire-irons and axes." Angèle walked across the hearth toward a small pile of supplies the group had carried with them.

"What are you doing?" Patrick asked.

"Looking for our spare bottles of rum," Angèle called back. "To make improvised grenades."

"We best be going then," said the Baron to Aoife. "I have no interest in watching this game play out. I presume that we shall see them in Guinee soon enough." Aoife agreed and placed her hand in his. The two of them vanished from the room, leaving Patrick and Cumberland alone to forge the weapons of their escape.

## Chapter 10

# Glut

"The banshee said she mourns us all," Cumberland pointed out.

"Aoife," said Patrick in her defense. "She did."

"So why are we marching toward our inevitable deaths?" Cumberland asked. "We could just hole up in the lighthouse, signal a passing ship—"

"Even if we could signal a ship, we'd still have to get down to the water. And as far as I can tell, the only way down is back through the woods and into the gorge, or we jump," Patrick said. "Our odds of surviving the jump or the woods are the same. Nil."

"Without Aoife in the lighthouse, it's likely that neither the wendigo nor his pukwudgie will remain confined to the woods," Angèle added. "They will get in."

"So, we're going on the offensive?" Cumberland said, clearly upset by the decision that had been made—though there was no second choice.

"That's the idea," Angèle said. "Though, I do wish Absalom and Thomas were with us."

"And the sisters," Patrick said.

"Yes," said Angèle, "and the sisters."

"What do you think happened to them?" Cumberland asked. No one responded.

The group had reached the gorge precipice, and upon their arrival an eerie moan began to emanate from below, like the aftershock of an earthquake working its way toward the surface. They all looked over the edge at the crooked river below and spotted a figure moving spasmodically along the bank before disappearing into a cave.

"What was that?" Cumberland exclaimed. "Was that it?"

"Could be," Angèle confirmed.

"I don't think so. It's hard to distinguish from this high up, but it looked to me like a trapped buck," Patrick estimated. "But how would it have gotten there?"

"The forest may be moving—closing in around us," Angèle deduced. "It's unsettling that we haven't yet encountered the pukwudgie."

"We can't be sure that their magic isn't working on us right now," Patrick said, "but whatever that was down there, it was too big to be a faery."

"It had antlers," Cumberland added to Patrick's theory that it was a panicked buck.

"Whatever it was, it seemed shaken. We had best keep moving. We don't want to face a wendigo shuffling single-file along the edge of a cliff," Angèle said and started into the deep gorge along the sinuous path before them. The trail was slick with ice so the three had to work their way toward the bottom with slow, assured steps. Cumberland and Patrick both used their fire-irons to steady themselves, while Angèle relied upon a walking stick fashioned from a branch that she found in the woods. They relinquished their worry to silence as they journeyed deeper into the gorge. A fog crept up, obscuring their view of where they were going and where they had been.

"I don't like this," Angèle was saying, when a wider trail emerged from a split in the rock face. The fog hadn't pierced the strange passageway, allowing them to assess the path whose snow was trampled into grey slush by human-like footprints.

"What do you think made those," Cumberland asked.

"We may have found the pukwudgie," said Patrick. "Look here, though. I wonder what they're dragging."

"Tails," Angèle said.

"I guess we're headed the right way, then?" Patrick said.

"It's unlikely the pukwudgie would attack us outright, Angèle said. They're clever and malicious, to be sure, but they're also not very brave."

They moved cautiously into the unusual channel. Angèle paused to wrap a shredded length of cloth around the end of her walking stick, which she then lit with a flint and steel and held out before her like a weaponized torch. In her left hand, she carried a jar of rum with a small scrap of cloth sticking out from beneath the lid, which she could ignite with the torch when necessary. Patrick and Cumberland waited for Angèle to lead the way through what turned out to be a complex series of passages. Before long, they were all disoriented by the numerous turns and branching passageways that all looked identical.

Smooth, stone slabs towering fifteen feet high on either side trapped them in a dizzying maze. It had evidently been built to lure its victims toward an inescapable center—but by whom or what? To keep his mind from brooding upon Daedalus's labyrinth at Knossos, and the Minotaur of King Minos who stalked its center, Patrick talked of his plans to settle in the Bronx with his uncle, "He's working on the Croton Aqueduct," he said to Cumberland. "I'm going to join his crew."

"Yeah, sure," Cumberland said, unconvinced of their escape.

"I can probably get you a job as well," he said. "Have you heard of Alexander Cartwright and the New York Knickerbockers?"

"No," Cumberland muttered, trying to pay attention to the path ahead of him.

"The last letter I received from my Uncle Pete described a game called 'baseball' that was invented not far from here, in Cooperstown, by a Military Academy cadet named Abner Doubleday. Rory and I used to pour over my uncle's letter that depicted a match between the New York Nine and the Knickerbockers in June 1846, just trying to imagine what the game looked like."

Each step felt to Cumberland like a nail being driven into his coffin. And the only reason he had been able to trek so deep into that maze in the first place was that he was too scared to turn back on his own. After listening to Patrick ramble for the better part of an hour, Cumberland said, "Maybe we could fortify the lighthouse."

"With Aoife gone the lighthouse is no longer safe. It may not have been safe with her there either. Somehow four people disappeared without us knowing where they went or how they left," Angèle said.

"Do you think Aoife was in on it?" Cumberland wondered.

"No," Patrick said. "She could have gotten rid of me any number of times. Hell, she didn't have to grant me entry in the first place. Why harbor a refugee if you're just planning to feed him to a monster?"

"Look! There!" Angèle pointed to a well at the center of intersecting trails.

As they approached, Patrick ran ahead to investigate the structure. "It's obviously man-made," he reported. He cautiously peered over the edge. When he looked into the well, his body relaxed. Patrick stood upright and placed his hands on the edge so that he could get a precise look inside the structure.

"What is it?" Angèle asked, intrigued by his body language.

"It's...odd. I was expecting it to be deep, but it looks to be, maybe, a ten-foot drop. And I think—" he leaned over the edge, straining to see to the depths below, "I think I can see an offshoot tunnel at the bottom. It is a bit dark, though; could just be shadows."

Angèle pulled Patrick back from the edge. She then ignited a piece of paraffin-soaked cloth and dropped it into the well. She and Patrick jockeyed for position around the small opening to see inside. "There's definitely some kind of a tunnel down there," Angèle reported.

"I suppose we ought to see where it leads," Patrick said.

"We're not going down there," Cumberland said. "It's surely a trap!"

"Could be," Patrick agreed.

"We've already been funneled into these narrow

passageways that have us all turned around, and now you want to go underground where our options for retreat are fewer," Cumberland contended.

"I wouldn't say that we *want* to go down there," Patrick admitted.

Angèle lit another piece of cloth, this time a strand attached to one of her jars filled with rum. She quickly dropped the jar into the well before it exploded in her hand. The group fell back a few paces and seconds later, when it had burst against the floor, a rush of heat shot up out of the well. "I think we can assume that same blast torched anything near the entryway of the tunnel. That should buy us a little time, at least," she assured Cumberland.

"Alright, who's going in first?" he conceded.

"I'll do it," said Patrick. He hopped up onto the ledge, swung his legs into the well and lowered himself down until he was hanging from the stone lip. Only a few feet from the ground, he let go of the rim and landed lightly on his feet. "Okay, I'm going in," he called up, then disappeared into the darkness.

Once all three of them had descended into the well and entered the subterranean tunnels, Cumberland couldn't help but point out that they had no way of returning to the surface: "I still think we've been tricked into this pit."

\* \* \*

Angèle, Patrick, and Cumberland wandered farther beneath the earth, to the point where oxygen had become thin. Their only light came from the dimming flame of Angèle's torch. The tunnel system had widened into a vast, circular room that the meager light could not fully illuminate. The glow that it did emit cast only a small circle of light around the group, making it impossible for them to see into the shadows. "What is this place?" Cumberland asked. "It doesn't look natural."

"You're right," Patrick said, running his hand over the smoothed rock. "It might be a coal mine."

"In the middle of the Adirondack wilderness?" said Angèle, doubtful.

"Possibly. It would be easy enough to ship south along the Hudson River into New York City or north along the Richelieu into Montreal," said Patrick. "If it is a mine, there should be an exit to the water somewhere. Maybe we'll reach the lake after all." Patrick paused. Then he said, "I wonder. It might actually belong to the United States Military. Captain McCawley of the *Agnes* told me to keep an eye out for Fort Ticonderoga, at the southern tip of Lake Champlain, in the event I needed to replenish my supplies. I'm not certain how far we've walked, nor if we've been moving in a straight line, but the gorge definitely runs to the south, so maybe we are alongside the lake."

"But, if this is a mine, then where are all the workers?" Cumberland asked.

"There," Angèle said, pointing to a pile of bones that had just become visible within the perimeter of light cast by her torch. The skeletons lay beyond a wooden archway that led into a small alcove just off the main chamber that appeared to be some sort of junction, given the number of tunnels converging upon the subterranean lyceum. "That arch proves that it was likely a coal mine at one time, but it's a wendigo lair now."

"Yeah," Patrick agreed, "but where is the wendigo?" He gripped tight his fire iron, ready for the creature to emerge at any moment.

"Hopefully asleep," Angèle said.

The low rumble of thunder rolled through the tunnels and into the circular room. It was impossible to decipher from which tunnel it emanated as it echoed off the anthracite walls. "I think we had better get out of here," Cumberland suggested. The group turned to retreat into the tunnel behind them that would lead back to the surface, but before they could reach it the opening collapsed.

"Come on," Patrick screamed to the others so that they could hear him above the shifting rock. He darted for the tunnel entrance nearest the pile of miner's bones with Angèle and Cumberland close behind him. Once through the wooden arch, the tunnel pitched further into the earth, dropping at an angle that made it difficult for the companions to slow their pace had they wanted to, but their only thought was to escape the lair before it collapsed upon them. As they descended, the rumble dissipated until they were completely out of earshot. "I don't think that was an earthquake," Patrick puffed when they finally came to a stop on a level section of ground.

"Nor I. We best keep moving," Angèle suggested. "Something is driving us further from the surface. We may have to fight our way out of here."

As Cumberland breathed deeply to collect himself after the scare, he noticed something out of place in the underground cavern. "I can smell the forest," he announced.

With their sense of smell trained on detecting any hint of vegetation, Angèle and Patrick soon found that they, too, could perceive the distinct scent of pine trees. "We must be close to an opening!" Patrick exclaimed and took off in the direction they had been heading without waiting for Angèle to light the way. Before long, the three of them had exited the caves at the bottom of the gorge near where they had witnessed the panicked buck bounding along the riverbank.

"This looks familiar," Cumberland said.

"Yes," Angèle agreed. "It seems that for all the traveling we've done today that we have ended up nearly where we began."

"The wendigo must be using the mines to traverse the forest," Patrick said.

"That mound of bones sure seemed too high to be only miners' bodies," Cumberland said.

"That mound of bones is likely 200 years old," Angèle said.

"If that's the case, portions of those tunnels must have been dug by the wendigo. There wasn't anyone here to mine in the 1640s," Patrick said.

"Do you think it has the pukwudgie lure its prey down there?" asked Cumberland, "That we—"

"Shh. Listen," Angèle said, holding out her arms to quiet the others.

Patrick and Cumberland closed their eyes as if to sharpen their hearing. Patrick cocked his head. "I don't hear anything."

"Not even crickets," Angèle said ominously.

"Not the water, either," Cumberland added, "but it's right there!"

"This is not good," Patrick said. A long moan echoed through the gorge, followed by a putrid and inescapable sulfuric stench that reminded Patrick of spoiled eggs. The group staggered backward and shielded their noses from the smell.

"It knows we're here," Angèle said.

"It brought us here!" Cumberland countered, and fled in the direction of the lighthouse.

The wendigo, as if moving at will between time and space, appeared from some unseen distance before Cumberland, blocking his path. Cumberland hadn't even time to flinch before the creature lashed out with its elongated fingers and obsidian-sharp talons. Its claws sliced into Cumberland's ribs as easily as a skipped stone would pierce a thin film of algae floating atop a tranquil pond. The boy screamed in agony, and Angèle ran to his side while Patrick's mind reeled. He thought about lunging forward with his silver-plated fire-iron aimed at the wendigo's heart, but before he could spring into action, the creature reached out with its preternaturally long arms and grabbed Patrick by the head. In one motion, the wendigo wrapped its long fingers around Patrick's skull and twisted until his neck snapped free from his spine. Following the sickening crack, the wendigo disappeared with its kill into the pines above Angèle and the unconscious boy to feast on Patrick's remains.

"We've got to get out of here," Angèle said aloud to motivate herself to act. When she tried to lift Cumberland, his eyes shot open with a flash of pain before he blacked out once again. Blood pulsed from his wound, staining Angèle's white djellaba. "Cumberland, if you can hear me, I've got to stop the bleeding right now. I'm going to cauterized your wound with the torch," she warned before pressing the flame to his body. The heat seared his skin, melting shut the wound. Cumberland showed no sign of response. His breath was shallow, and his heartbeat slow, but he was still alive.

Knowing that she had little time remaining before the wendigo finished its meal and returned for her and Cumberland, Angèle hoisted the dying boy on her back and secured his body to hers using a kitenge, and began the trek back to the lighthouse. With each onerous step, she panted out a prayer to Belie Belcan, lwa of justice and defender against malevolent forces.

Belie Belcan,

defend us in battle.

Be our protection against the wickedness and snares of the devil's kin.

May God rebuke him, I humbly pray;

and do Thou, O Prince of the Heavenly Host,

by the Divine Power of God,

cast into hell Satan and all the evil spirits

who roam throughout the world seeking the ruin of souls.

When Angèle reached the gorge wall, having no alternative, she climbed. Every inch of her ascent was a struggle: her limbs became bruised, and her hands bled where the skin had worn away from her mangled fingertips. Each time she let go of the rock face to position her hand higher, the weight of Cumberland on her back threatened to pull them away from the cliff and send them plummeting to their deaths.

"Help!" Patrick called. "Angèle, Help me!"

She paused, her arms shaking from the weight she was forcing them to hold. Angèle slowly turned her head away from the wall to peer across the treetops.

"Please!" Patrick begged. His voice echoed against the cliffs sounding as if he were in multiple places at the same time.

"No," Angèle said to reassure herself that she had made the right decision to escape with Cumberland, "you dead." Having seen the wendigo spin Patrick's head one hundred and eighty degrees on his shoulders, and recalling the crackling of his spine that had sent a shiver down her own, Angèle knew that those cries for help were not Patrick's, but the wendigo using mimicry in an attempt to lure her back into the forest. She pressed on.

Within a few body lengths of the top, Angèle had reached a ledge and paused to allow her arm muscles to recover. She released Cumberland from the kitenge to check his wounds. Pulling back his coat, and separating the folds of his torn shirt, Angèle saw that most of the burns had miraculously begun scarring. In some places, even the scar tissue had fully healed. Angèle quickly thanked Baron Samedi for intervening to stave off Cumberland's death, then turned her attention back to the forest, scanning the treetops and the depths of the gorge for any sign of the wendigo.

The forest was still except for the leisurely flow of the river below. But this was the sort of predatory stillness that erupts into a menace with the momentum of a plunging guillotine. Perhaps, Angèle thought, the creature was waiting for nightfall to return. The sunlight had already streaked the sky pink and orange, and the deep purple of dusk was soon to follow. Though she hadn't gotten a clean look at the beast as it claimed Patrick, the image of its enormous, sunken, red eyes flashing at her with unbridled evil, and its yellowed, needlelike fangs projecting from its stinking maw haunted her memory. The wendigo was bigger than she had expected—twice the size of the man it used to be—especially given the speed with which it closed in upon them.

Fearing the encroaching dark, Angèle positioned herself to once again strap Cumberland to her back for the final stretch of the arduous climb. She moved him gingerly, propping his back against the rock face so that he was sitting upright. Cumberland groaned and stretched his bones, causing his joints to grind and pop. "Don't move too much," Angèle said, excited that he was conscious. "We should dress your wounds."

Cumberland nodded, and Angèle carefully removed his shirt so that she could bandage his torso. Cumberland opened his jaundiced eyes to assess the damage. His brow knitted in confusion when he saw that his skin bore no mark. He looked into Angèle's equally astonished face and asked, "How?"

"The Baron," said Angèle, smiling at Cumberland. "Do you think you can climb?" she pressed.

"I think so," Cumberland said, and stood to test his legs.

"Good thing," Angèle admitted, "I'm not sure I could have made it the rest of the way."

"I can't believe you made it this far," he said, looking down the steep cliff. He searched the ledge, realizing Patrick was no longer with them. "Patrick?"

"Didn't make it," Angèle said.

Cumberland took a deep breath to bury his feelings and prepare himself for the climb ahead. He looked up at the ridge, twenty or so feet above them, and, grasping his stomach, said, "I'm starved."

"Do you have the energy to make it?" Angèle asked.

Cumberland nodded and placed a hand on the wall to begin his climb.

"Hang on. I'm going to lob one of these rum grenades up and over the ledge to make sure it's clear of any pukwudgie that could be waiting for us," Angèle said.

"Good idea," Cumberland agreed.

Angèle sparked her flint against the rock, igniting one of the rum-soaked shards of fabric. The instant a flame erupted from the cloth, Cumberland shrieked in horror and lurched backward with such force that he lost his footing and careened off the ledge. Angèle, whose back was to him as she was in the act of throwing the jar over the cliff, recoiled at the sound of his inhuman scream. She dropped the bomb as her hands flew to cover her ears. The ledge upon which she rested was high enough that Angèle had time to turn and see Cumberland's body flailing through the air before he hit the ground.

Her grenade struck the earth a second later. It shattered, producing a muffled explosion. The fire erupted not far from Cumberland's body, though not close enough to ignite his clothes. Cumberland's scream called to mind that of the wendigo in the catacombs, confirming that his body's regeneration was not the work of the Baron, but the result of having been infected by the wendigo's curse.

Angèle scrambled to the surface and looked back once more at the gorge floor before retreating to the lighthouse. Cumberland was gone.

# 11

# Chapter 11

# (Dis)Belief

"What is that?" Emily asked. The sisters had both sat down on the bed to wait for the others to return from above.

"What?" Mary said, looking around the room.

"There, on the wall," Emily said. She pointed to where the headboard had been before they had helped Patrick push the bed beneath the hatch so that he could climb through to the lantern gallery.

"That is odd. It almost looks like a doorway—it's the same type of stone as the others, but it's definitely cut differently," Mary said.

"Do you really think someone did that on purpose?" Emily asked. "Perhaps it leads into a crawlspace."

"It might," Mary agreed. "It certainly looks like it should move, but wouldn't the exterior of the lighthouse be on the other side of this wall?"

"I suppose. Shall we try it?" Emily asked.

"If it is a storage space, we might find something useful in there," Mary suggested with a shrug.

The two women slid from the bed to inspect the strange stone. It was no more than three feet high by two feet wide. It was perfectly smooth, unlike the surrounding wall. "There doesn't seem to be any way to open it," Emily said to Mary, trying unsuccessfully to wedge her fingertips in the small space between the panel and the stone wall.

"Can you push it?" Mary asked.

Emily leaned her shoulder into the slab, but it did not budge. "It doesn't appear so," she said.

"Well, that is curious, isn't it," said Mary. "Maybe it's a load-bearing stone, and that's why it's so big."

"I hadn't thought of that," Emily admitted and sat back on her heels. "I guess we can ask Patrick and Angèle what they think when they come back down." She reached out a hand to use the wall for support as she picked herself up from the ground, then offered her other hand to Mary. As she pulled Mary up, Emily casually grasped a wall sconce for balance. It tilted forward with a click, and the stone panel dropped into the floor. "Now that's curious," Emily said.

Mary had already dropped back to her knees and peered inside.

"What is it? What do you see?" Emily asked, excited.

"I don't know," Mary said. "It's too dark." She reached her arm in to see what she could feel. "Stairs!" she reported, "spiraling down."

"There must be an interstice between the interior bedroom wall and the exterior façade," Emily said.

"Yes, but why?" her sister asked, crawling into the space. "Emily, get a candle from the dresser."

"You're not going in there," Emily said uneasily.

"We should at least see where it goes," Mary said. "We are looking for a way out of here, remember."

"It goes down," Emily said, feeling the grip of claustrophobia begin to tighten around her at even the thought of squeezing into a narrow cavity between the walls.

"Yes, but for what purpose?" Mary wondered. "I can go by myself if you'd prefer—"

"You'd leave me here alone?" Emily said, a note of distress in her voice. She gathered a candle and saucer from the dresser and pushed her sister into the hidden stairwell so that she could squeeze in behind her. Once both women were inside the walls, they maneuvered so that they could stand up, albeit in a severely crouched position.

"It's pretty cramped in here. We'll have to walk single-file. I'll go first," Mary offered. She took the candle from her sister and began to make her way down the stairs with Emily close behind.

When Mary's foot landed on the third step, the panel slammed shut behind them.

Emily panicked and let out an anguished cry. She spun around to claw at the panel. "Are we trapped?" she shouted to her sister.

Mary put a calming hand on Emily's back, "Let's just take the stairs down to wherever it is they lead. Maybe there is an exit somewhere."

"I didn't see any other hidden doorways downstairs, did you?" Emily asked, her nerves raw.

"No," Mary said, trying to remain calm, "but we weren't looking for any, either." She hooked her sister's arm, "Come with me—we're going to be fine. The worst that will happen is that we'll have to wait for the others to climb down from the lantern gallery and notice we're missing. Surely, they'll find the hidden panel just as we did."

Emily's tensed muscles relaxed. "Okay," she said. "But if I hear them on the other side of the wall, I'm going to scream for help."

"Me, too," Mary agreed. "Let's go."

Bent at the waist and with hunched shoulders, the sisters descended the narrow staircase. Mary's candle lighted the way, but they were never sure what lurked beyond each bend. After a few minutes, the air became damp and warm. "I think we're underground," Mary said.

"Should we turn back?" Emily asked. "If we're no longer in the lighthouse, how will the others find us?"

"We could, though there might be a way out at the bottom," Mary suggested. "We can always turn back if we reach a dead end."

"Okay, if it means we don't have to traverse the woods," Emily agreed uneasily. They carried on, and the smooth walls and finished steps became rough and uneven as the sisters descended further beneath the earth. When the ground finally leveled out, the ceiling rose high above them, allowing the sisters to stand tall in the narrowing cavern that appeared to extend in a straight line for some distance.

"Are you alright," Mary asked her sister, who seemed to be on the verge of hyperventilating.

"I feel like the walls are closing in. I can't go on," she said.

"Here, sit down for a moment. I'm just going to walk a few paces down the corridor to see if the candlelight brings anything into focus. If you feel like I'm getting to be too far away, holler and I'll double back," Mary said.

Emily sat on the ground and took a deep breath, "As soon as I call, you had better turn around," she said.

"I will," Mary assured her and wandered into the shadows. They were in a straight shaft that was high enough for her to stand erect as she walked, but her arms were almost pinned at her sides because the walls were so close together. "It looks like someone built this," she called back to her sister.

"Yes, but for what purpose?" Emily yelled.

"I'm not sure," Mary said. She wondered why they wouldn't have widened the passageway. "It almost feels like I'm being funneled toward something," she said to herself before yelling back to Emily, "I'm just going to go a bit further then we can head back. The others might want to explore this as a potential escape route."

Before Emily could respond, the candlelight immediately disappeared, as if Mary had snuffed it out between her fingertips. Emily was left alone, cowering in complete darkness. "Mary!" she screamed. Her sister did not respond.

* * *

Emily lay in frozen terror on the stone floor. She pressed her cheek against the cool ground and spread wide her arms as if to steady herself in the face of a tumultuous bout of vertigo brought on by her claustrophobia. Unblinking, her panicked eyes searched the darkness for any sign of her sister. She wanted to run after Mary, but couldn't convince her paralyzed body to move. Instead, she contemplated the choices before her: return to the secret stairwell between the lighthouse walls and wait near the trick panel in hopes that Patrick, Angèle, or Cumberland would pass by and hear her frenzied pleas for help; or venture into the unknown blackness in pursuit of her sister and risk being drawn further from safety. Either way, Emily would have to move.

Though it felt to her like hours had passed since the candle flame had gone out and her sister disappeared from the corridor, Emily had been lying on the ground for only a few trepidatious minutes before she began to hear footsteps approaching from the stairwell. At first, she thought that she might be hallucinating, but the steady patter gave her hope that the footsteps belonged to one of her companions searching for the missing women. "We're here!" Emily called out. "Follow the stairs down to my voice!" When she had finished yelling she could hear that the footsteps had stopped, enfolding the cave in an impregnable silence. Emily wasn't sure what to make of the quiet, so she tried again, this time calling out to her friends by name. "Angèle! Cumberland!" No one responded. "Patrick!" Perhaps her mind had imagined the sound of rescuers; maybe she was alone. Then, the footsteps sounded again, though their noise had changed, or grown close enough that Emily could hear the nuanced scratching of claws scrambling to grip the slick stones beyond the bottom of the constructed stairs. It sounded, too, as if they had multiplied.

Possessed by fear, Emily leaped to her feet and lurched wildly down the path toward the spot where she had last seen Mary. Her heart pumped with such force as she sprinted away from the mysterious footsteps that its beating throbbed in her ears, blotting out all other sounds. She bound through the darkness, unable to see anything before her, yet unafraid of what was to come. Her only thought was to escape the skulking geist.

Emily ran headlong into a solid wall. Her face bounced off the stone, knocking out her front teeth and fracturing her nose. She crumpled to the ground but fought to retain consciousness. "Mary," she moaned. The creatures closed in on her.

A piercing ring overwhelmed the drumming of Emily's heartbeat in her ears, making it impossible for her to hear how close the clawed feet and menacing purrs had advanced. She was confident, though, that it was only a matter of seconds before they began to tear into her flesh. Tired and broken, she almost welcomed the end. To stop from choking on the blood pooling in her mouth, Emily rolled over to spit it out, which is when she inadvertently activated a floor switch that shifted the wall, delivering her at the candle-lighted feet of her sister.

"Oh, my dear!" Mary gasped. She immediately fell to the ground and cradled Emily's head in her lap. "What happened to you?"

"Monthster," Emily lisped through her broken teeth.

"What monster?" Mary asked.

"Faeries, I think," Emily said, trying to control her sobs.

"Okay, okay," Mary consoled her sister. "We're safe for the moment. Can you walk?"

Emily nodded. She had become less affected by her claustrophobia now that she was reunited with her sister. "Do you think they'll get through the wall?"

"I don't even know how we got through the wall," Mary said, and helped Emily to her feet.

"There's a panel on the ground. I accidentally rolled onto it when I was spitting up blood," Emily reported.

"Let's hope the pukwudgie don't trample on it, or know it's there," Mary said and tore a bit of fabric from her linsey-woolsey dress. She gave it to Emily to suck on. "Maybe that will help curb the bleeding until we can find help."

Emily accepted the cloth and Mary's arm; the two sisters

continued their flight through the underground cave, looking back every few paces to see if the wall had rotated again to let the pukwudgie through. With the melting candle held out before them, they raced on, waiting for the monotony of stone walls and uneven ground to come to a halt, which it did in the form of a fork in the tunnel. The sisters stopped.

"What now?" Emily asked.

"Left or right," Mary said.

"Your guess is as good as mine," said Emily.

"Should we split up—" Mary asked.

"No!" Emily insisted.

"Alright," Mary said, trying to calm her sister. "What if you stay here while I—"

"I said 'no,' Mary. Wherever you go, I go," Emily stated.

"Fair enough. Pick a tunnel," Mary said. They stood in silence, peering into the darkness. They first assessed the tunnel to the left, then the tunnel to the right. They listened for any hint of what may lie beyond the reach of the candle's weak flame. Finally, Mary admitted, "I don't think we're going to be able to make an educated guess."

"The spiraling of the staircase makes it impossible to know which direction we were facing when we left the lighthouse," Emily said with a great deal of pain. "But if I had to guess, I'd say the path to the left would take us into the mountains, meaning the tunnel leading to the right should deposit us near the lakeshore. Maybe."

"Okay, to the right it is," Mary said, and started them off in the direction they hoped would take them to the lake. The farther they traveled down the tunnel, the wilder their surroundings became. Stalactites hung from the ceiling and stalagmites seemed to erupt from the floor. The cave itself opened further into an expansive cavern, allowing the women to navigate around the rock deposits that had grown together to form columns in some places. The terrain looked as if it were a mouth filled with crooked fangs that threatened to close upon the sisters at any moment. They pressed on, each secretly hoping that the ceiling would not come crashing down.

The rhythmic sound of lapping waves eventually reached their ears, and the rank smell of rotting fish gave them both a jolt of optimistic energy. Small pools of water began to appear on the cavern floor where the high tide had stranded perch and trout on the rocks as evidence of its retreat. Mary and Emily soon found themselves knee-deep in a tide pool as they raced toward the sonorous surf.

* * *

Mary and Emily stood on a thin strip of pebbly beach just outside the cave entrance, waving frantically to the crew of a sidewheel steamer chugging south toward Lake George and, presumably, the Hudson River beyond. They screamed wildly, and their voices were carried on a westerly wind to the ears of the shipmen who quickly diverted their course to help the stranded women. As the boat approached the shore, Mary and Emily could hear the baying of wolves emanating from the cave behind them. The sisters plunged into the icy water for fear of the wolves attacking them before a lifeboat could be dispatched from the steamer. Energized by adrenaline, they swam through the deadly-cold slush toward the boat. The crew had thrown a pair of Kisbee rings into the water, and once the sisters had caught hold of them, Mary and Emily were hauled to the side of the boat, where a sailor clung to a rope ladder. He pulled Emily from the water first and passed her to the deckhands above. Next, he offered his hand to Mary. She took it, and the two of them climbed aboard the *Champlain Transportation Company* cargo-ferry.

"What the hell are you two doing out here?" The sailor asked Mary. He covered her with a woolen blanket and hugged her to him to share his body heat.

"We got lost in the woods," she said, unsure if she could trust the man with a more detailed story, but burying her freezing face into the crook of his neck.

A pack of seven wolves appeared from the cave to stalk the shoreline. "Looks like you found your way out of there in the nick of time!" said the sailor.

"Yes," Mary agreed, staring at the wolves from the safety of the boat. They paced along the beach in a show of agitation at having lost their prey, then disappeared into the cavern. Mary wondered if they were simply wolves starved by the frost and prowling for food, or if these were the shapeshifting pukwudgie. "Look!" she exclaimed and tugged at the sailor's shirt to focus his attention on the shadows just inside the cave. "Do you see their eyes? That yellow glow, it can't be natural!"

"It's probably the sunlight reflecting off of them," he said. "Wolves have a reflective lens that helps them to see better in the dark."

"No," Mary insisted. "Those are faery eyes!"

"What?" The sailor asked. "I think you might be in shock from the cold—"

"Faeries, pukwudgie. That's what was after us in the woods. Them and a wendigo."

"A What?" The sailor asked even more confused. When Mary didn't respond, he became sure that her mental state was as fragile as her shivering body. She might even be further suffering from malnutrition or sleep deprivation, he thought. "You runaways?" he asked.

"Yes, sir," Mary absentmindedly admitted, still staring into those glowing eyes.

"Alright, let's get you to a cabin. The ship's doctor is taking a look at your friend.

"Sister," Mary said.

"Alright, well, you're next," the sailor said. He picked her up as if she were nothing more than a small child. The cave disappeared into the distance as the ferry churned southward. Above it loomed the ruined lighthouse.

"We were there," Mary mumbled, mostly to herself.

"Split Rock?" The sailor laughed. "No one's been up there in years. I heard it's haunted."

"It is," Mary said gravely.

The sailor knitted his brow, shaken by her earnestness. "What do you mean, it is?"

Mary opened her mouth to explain, but couldn't find the words before a shriek ripped through the woods and across the lake water with such nefarious force that it blew the small steamboat off course.

"What the blazes was that?" the sailor asked.

One of his buddies who was eavesdropping on the strange conversation interjected, "I never heard of no animal could make a sound like that."

"The wendigo," Mary said. "It's on the hunt."

The two sailors looked at one another with disbelief. "Prolly just a bear," one man said.

"And that wind?" the other asked.

"Coincidence?" replied the first man.

"I'm telling you, there's a wendigo in those woods. And my friends are out there," Mary said.

"There's more of you?" the sailor asked, shocked. "Black or white?"

"Both," Mary said.

"George, we ain't goin' back," said the man who had pulled Mary from the water.

"I know, Charlie. But, the captain ought to hear this," George said.

"You're right," Charles concluded. "I'm going to take her to the medical cabin. Fetch the captain from the pilot house and meet me upstairs."

"Aye," said George, turning to climb the stairs to the hurricane deck.

"Okay, Miss. Let's get you inside. It looks like an ice storm is moving in behind that fog," Charles said.

"My name is Mary," she said, introducing herself to the man who pulled her from the lake.

"Well, okay, Mary. There's a warm bed with your name on it just down the way, here," Charles said. He had climbed the steps George had taken to retrieve the captain, and exited the stairwell onto the boiler deck. When they arrived at a door bearing a medical placard, Charles kicked it open and deposited Mary into the bed opposite her sister, who was asleep under a heavy comforter.

"Get those wet clothes off immediately," the doctor ordered Mary. "When you're ready, the steward brought up some oatmeal and hot whiskey from the kitchen. It's there on the end table."

"Thank you," Mary said, unaccustomed to such hospitality.

"We'll give you some privacy," the doctor said. "I'll be back up to check on you in a few minutes. He ushered Charles into the hallway and locked the door behind them.

"Is that necessary?" asked Charles.

"That woman is a raving lunatic," Dr. Stanton declared.

"Mary?" Charles said.

"The other one, Emily I think she said. Ghosts and shapeshifters and demons! It's absurd!" the doctor declared.

"I know, I know, but her sister said something similar. They couldn't both be delusional, could they?" Charles asked.

"Look here, I'm sure they're frightened and tired. They may be playing into one another's hysteria," the doctor speculated.

"Still, is it possible they've actually seen something?" Charles asked.

The doctor raised an eyebrow.

"What about them Fox sisters in Hydesville?" Charles pressed.

"Oh, not you too!" the doctor exclaimed. "Those Fox sisters

are as phony as the Salem witches."

"Do you think they're running a con, or are they suffering from some sort of hallucination?" Charles wondered.

"Perhaps both," the doctor speculated. "It could be they believe their own nonsense."

"I agree, doctor," said Captain Silas, who had just arrived alongside George. "Still, I'd like to know what those women were doing up at Split Rock. That lighthouse is condemned."

"How would they have even got there?" Charles asked.

"Must have traversed the Adirondacks," George guessed.

"I wouldn't be surprised if they had a chaperone. The abolitionists are active in these parts," Captain Silas added. "Probably making their way to Nova Scotia."

"There are easier routes," Charles said.

"The one of 'em did mention others," said George.

"Bah! She's mad," Dr. Stanton assured them. "And I'm not sure the other one will survive her trauma. We best get them to Blackwell's straight away."

"Indeed," the captain said, reassuring Dr. Stanton. He turned to call on one of the deckhands, "George."

"Yes, sir?"

"Run upstairs and tell Jeffries to bypass Albany; set course for Manhattan.

"Yes, sir."

"The East River, George."

"Yes, sir. Port?"

"The Octagon."

\* \* \*

"I don't envy them this," Charles said as he and George helped Dr. Stanton wheel the sedated women down the stage and onto the small island. A vacant boathouse welcomed them. Presumably someone would be there to greet the visiting families of the insane, should any such appointment be made.

"Aye," said George solemnly, taking in the gloom of the place. A cold fog enveloped them, and the weeping willows—sure to be beautiful in the springtime—languished about the frozen yard. "D'ye remember that fellow, a bigshot writer, I think, with your same name, toured this place in '42? And his wife, Catherine was it? How'd you describe her?"

"I do," Charles said, recalling the man. "I think that was the last time I docked here."

"Remember what he said about them lunatics?" George pressed.

"To the word," Charles said, staring up at the massive mental hospital from the boathouse steps. The Octagon sat in the middle of the island with three-story wings flanking out to the east and south, obscuring their view of Queens. "Everything had a lounging, listless, madhouse air, which was very painful. The moping idiot, cowering down with long disheveled hair; the gibbering maniac, with his hideous laugh and pointed finger; the vacant eye, the fierce, wild face, the gloomy picking of the hands and lips, and munching of the nails: there they were all, without disguise, in naked ugliness and horror."[9]

"That's it," George said. "I'll be leaving the missus at the door, thank you very much."

"Relax, George. The orderlies will take them indoors," Dr. Stanton said, calming the man's nerves. "The health commission wouldn't even let me inside."

"Kinda makes you wonder what they're hiding," said George.

"I think Charles's recitation just about covers it," the doctor responded.

The ground was hard, but the weight of Mary and Emily in their wheelchairs cracked iced-over puddles and dredged ruts into the quadrangle from the river to the five-story rotunda. They were met beneath the main entryway doors by two male orderlies clad in white who took the women into their custody without a word. A nurse, joyless and stern, immediately began checking the sisters' vital signs and recorded her incriminating notes with amusement.

Dr. Stanton conferred with the chief psychiatrist and medical director, Dr. James McDonald about the transfer and care of the women. He related the sisters' tale of Split Rock and their claims of supernatural activity. "Not to worry, we've seen this sort of thing before," Dr. McDonald chortled. He threw his elbow into the ribs of Dr. Stanton to prod a bit of laughter from his colleague. Dr. McDonald then removed his spectacles and cleaned them with a monogrammed handkerchief pulled from his lab coat pocket. When he set the glasses back upon his nose, Dr. McDonald was delighted to see Dr. Stanton forcing what he interpreted as a worried smile of uncertainty.

"We are going to attend to their every need, doctor," Dr. McDonald said, clapping Dr. Stanton on the back. "Isn't that right nurse?"

"Absolutely," she affirmed without looking up from her paperwork.

"If you'll excuse me, gentlemen, I have rounds to make," Dr. McDonald said with a crooked smile.

"Of course," Dr. Stanton said, "we wouldn't want to keep you from caring for your patients."

"Indeed," said the doctor, squeezing the nurse as he entered the rotunda. Her lips curled into a grin, and she followed him through the double doors.

George pulled Dr. Stanton aside, and the orderlies pushing Mary and Emily filed in behind the nurse, "Are you certain we ought to be leaving the missus here," he asked.

"No," Dr. Stanton said, drawing out each letter in a prolonged admission, as if the consequences of his answer were sinking in as he spoke.

"We can't take them with us," Charles chimed in. "They got no use on the boat. And while I'm no abolitionist, I ain't brining home any slaves neither."

The steel door slammed shut, damning Mary and Emily to a miserable refuge for their trouble. The institution was surely undeserving of the name asylum in those ostensibly enlightened days.

Dr. Stanton raised his eyebrows begrudgingly as if to say, "That settles it, then." He ordered the sailors back to their ferry: "Come along. The captain will be expecting us. We've got a schedule to keep."

"Yes, sir," the men said in unison. They turned their backs upon the New York Lunatic Asylum and began their trudge across the lawn, toward the dock. None of them once looked back.

When they had sufficiently retreated across the quadrangle, and Dr. McDonald was certain that they would not return, he flicked closed a brass cover to hide the eyehole that he had personally drilled in the main door when he was appointed Overseer General. He then slid shut a series of vertical deadbolts and slide locks that played a familiar concert of sounds that roused Mary from her stupor.

Her eyes shot open and flitted around the great hall. Mary wondered if she were having another nightmare, but when she tried to stand, she found that she was restrained to a bath chair. Mary began to rock violently in an attempt to free herself, but the two back wheels, and the one front wheel, seemed to be locked in place. She could hear the sounds of water running, not like a stream or the surf, but of a fountain twinkling. Before her rose a grand staircase that climbed to a height beyond what her blurred vision could see. She thought that she could make out people moving up and down the stairs, but laudanum had made her severely groggy so she couldn't be sure. Mary called out for her sister, "Emily!"

"Your sister is still asleep," a man's voice informed her. Mary craned her neck as far as she could in either direction in an attempt to see behind her. She began to worry that this was not a nightmare and that what she had dreamed—likely under the influence of opium she had been coerced to smoke—was her flight from the Turk's brothel and subsequent ride on the underground railroad into the cursed woods. She was unsure which reality she preferred.

"Mehmed?" Mary said.

"I'm sorry, who is Mehmed?" the voice asked.

"Uhgn. Where am I?" Mary asked. She massaged her temples with the tips of her fingers, then pressed them against her closed eyes.

"Where do you think you are?" the voice asked.

"LePrete," she said.

"And what is that?" asked the voice.

"Um. A house," Mary said.

"Do you work at this house?"

"No. Yes, Mary said, confused. "We are all slaves."

"Indeed," said the voice.

"I dreamed we had escaped," Mary continued.

"Why do you think that your escape was a dream?" the voice asked.

"Here we are," said Mary, trying to gesture at the mansion's great hall. She laughed, a small, disappointed sound.

"Do you find something funny?" the man asked.

"I'm pretty sure we used magic to flee this place. I should have known it was a dream. To be honest, that's not even the strangest part of our tale," Mary said.

"Oh? Are you a witch?" asked the voice.

"No."

"Your sister, then?" the voice inquired.

"No. Angèle is a witch," Mary admitted.

"And who is Angèle?" the voice requested.

"She is gone," Mary stated. "Gone."

"Of course," the voice concluded. Mary could then hear the

man murmuring instructions to another who also stood behind her, outside of her field of vision. "Let's get these women admitted and into the sixth ward—"

"Dementia?" the nurse asked.

"I'm afraid so," Dr. McDonald said. "Separate rooms."

"No," Mary said.

"Let's schedule this one for a bloodletting within the hour," Dr. McDonald continued, placing his hands on Mary's shoulders and ignoring her plea to remain with her sister. "Cryotherapy for the other one..." Dr. McDonald paused to look at the nurse's file, "Emily."

"Yes, doctor," the nurse said and scribbled on her notepad.

"You can't separate us! Emily is not well," Mary cried.

"My dear, you are not well," the doctor declared.

"What?" Mary asked, surprised.

Dr. McDonald continued his instructions to the nurse, "Telegraph Dr. Litchfield at Bloomingdale. He's been experimenting with an anticonvulsant sedative that may help us manage this one."

"James—" the nurse began.

"What is it?" asked the doctor.

"Some of the nurses at Bloomingdale have been talking. Nearly all of Litchfield's patients have committed suicide after being dosed with his drugs," the nurse warned.

"Gossip!" Dr. McDonald shouted. "Now, get Litchfield here. And pray we don't dose you!"

"Yes, doctor," the nurse capitulated and scurried off down the hallway.

The orderlies pushed the bath chairs in her wake. Mary screamed for the orderlies to stop, but they continued mechanically down the dark corridor until they reached a wooden platform enclosed by thick beams. The orderlies pushed the sisters' chairs onto the platform behind the nurse and pulled shut a security beam.

"What is this thing?" Mary demanded.

"An ascending room. Nothing to be afraid of," said the nurse. An operator shoveled coal as black as his skin into a furnace next to the steam engine, which began rotating a leather belt that pulled on a counterweight, lifting the platform into the air.

"Help me!" Mary begged the operator as the platform began to rise, taking her far above his head. She craned her neck over the edge to see the man as long as she could. Once his figure had disappeared far below her, she prayed under her breath, "Help me."

The lift came to a stop, and the orderlies wheeled Mary and Emily down another long corridor and into their separate rooms. "Can't I stay with my sister? At least until she wakes up?" Mary asked.

"Your sister has suffered great facial trauma. We're going to treat her as best we can, and we'll bring you to see her if she regains consciousness," the nurse assured her. "In the meantime, it's clear that you are suffering from the result of some emotional distress—likely linked to your sister's condition. It's best for you to have a bit of time alone."

"What do you mean, if? Will Emily live?" Mary asked frantically.

Before Mary knew what was happening, the nurse had pressed a small, innocuous-looking brass box against her forearm and released a spring-loaded lever at the top causing twelve short blades to create a series of shallow cuts in her flesh. Mary winced and tried to recoil from the pain, but her arms had been tightly bound to the chair.

"Why am I tied down," she demanded to know. The nurse simply reloaded the device and shifted to Mary's other arm as blood began to collect in a drip-pan from the initial wounds.

"Please, not again. One is enough!" Mary cried. "It hurts!"

"Doctor's orders," the nurse said, releasing the lever for the second time. Mary wept. "Only two more to go," the nurse assured her. But, before the nurse could administer the third round of cuts, this time located upon her patient's upper thigh, Mary fainted. "Ah, working already. The sleep will do you a world of good, dear," the nurse said happily and finished her work uninterrupted.

* * *

When Mary awoke, she found herself alone in her room. She was reclined in the bath chair, but her restraints had been removed, along with the stainless-steel drip pans. A stained mattress made of shoddy and filled with straw ticks lay behind her. The walls and ceilings were whitewashed with lime. No windows invited outside light nor offered Mary views of the ornate grounds. As far as she could tell, the plain room measured nine feet long by five feet wide and was lighted by a miserable little, barred peephole of about one foot in diameter. It looked out through the cell door on the west side of the room and into a barren hallway.

Mary stood, using the chair's armrests for support. The cuts on her arms had already begun to scab over, indicating that she had likely been unconscious for hours—maybe as long as a day. The stiffness in her leg muscles and her obstinate joints seemed to confirm that estimate. Her mouth was dry and tasted foul. She licked her cracked lips as she labored to walk from the middle of the room to the doorway, a distance of no more than three paces. With luck, Mary managed to stumble into the door and catch herself on the bars before toppling to the floor. Hauling her feet back underneath her, Mary inadvertently knocked them against an unnoticed pewter bedpan, and rose to her full height to peer through the hole into the hallway. The corridor was lighted by kerosene lamps placed at regular intervals of about every ten feet. This meant that she was able to see two lamps, one in either direction—her door being equidistant from each.

"Emily," she tried softly, so as not to attract the attention of the hospital staff. The scratch in her throat was irritating, but when her sister did not respond she tried again in a harsh whisper, "Emily." A cockroach skittered along the darkened baseboard until it disappeared into a gap in the floor opposite her door. With no response forthcoming from her sister's room, which she assumed to be adjacent to her own, she called out to anyone who might respond. "Hello?" Only the echo of her own voice answered from the empty hall, and Mary began to fear the worst. She pounded her fist against the wooden door. "I'm awake," she yelled, "and thirsty. May I have some water?" She counted in her head to thirty before trying again, "Please, may I see my sister? Let me out of here!" The weight of her solitude pressed down upon her like a salacious incubus. "Anybody!" she howled into the vacant ward.

# Chapter 12

# Immured

Angèle braced herself against the whipping wind. Sleet stung her face. She raised her arms before her to shield herself against the anomalous ice storm that had blown across the lake and into the valley, slowing her retreat. The lighthouse should have been in her sights, but a freezing fog had settled at the base of Cloven Rock Mountain, obscuring the unlit, desolate tower. The gale intensified with each aggravated growl that exploded from the cursed woods, and hail pellets began to hurtle from the flocculent gray of the heaped storm clouds.

"Angèle! Wait for me!" A scared voice beseeched from within the fog.

"Cumberland," Angèle gasped. She stopped dead in her tracks and turned to look for the boy. The opaque gloom—and the trees that had once again closed in around Angèle—obscured his figure. "It's here! Don't leave me! I don't want to die!" Eyes like molten gold burned through the dense fog—the wendigo stood at the edge of the gorge.

Angèle, knowing Cumberland must have died in the fall, turned from the creature. She had only a meager head start, considering the speed at which the wendigo had proven it could close distances. She ran toward what she hoped would be the safety of the lighthouse, creating a straight line of deep tracks in the fresh snow. In a flash of luck, lightning split the sky, and Angèle saw for a moment the brass vent ball gleam atop the lighthouse cupola towering above the forest to her left. She nearly dropped her pack of improvised grenades to pick up speed, but thought better of it and adjusted her course northward with the bag still slung over her shoulder. Holding the soggy hem of her dress up above her knees with one hand, and the jostling sack in the other, Angèle bound through the snow like a startled deer evading an eager mountain lion. Still, she could sense the creature closing in on her. When she arrived at the clearing, Angèle gambled a look behind her to see how much ground the wendigo had made up, but it was nowhere to be seen. Certain that she hadn't lost the creature and that this was part of its hunting tactics, Angèle bolted through the heavy door and into the confines of the empty lighthouse. She dropped a lock-bar across the door behind her and withdrew into the center of the room, near the table where she and her companions had told one another their unlikely stories of survival.

Angèle crawled beneath the table to where Patrick and Cumberland had deposited her wooden trunk. She unclasped the decorative silver latch and pulled back the heavy lid, inviting Damballa from her nest. The snake raised its head from deep within its coils to see who had dared disturb her slumber. At the sight of Angèle, Damballa relaxed, flicked her tongue and slithered around the woman's shoulders.

"Mama," Angèle said, convoking the spirit of her mother to possess the snake. Furious shouts penetrated the crumbling stone walls. The reverberations shook the lighthouse on its foundation—dust rained down from the decayed ceiling. The wendigo had arrived; there were two of them.

"Angèle, let me in!" one of the creatures cried using Cumberland's voice.

"Mama!" Angèle urged, this time with a sting of annoyance. She traced the sign of the Christian cross upon the snake's head then dashed from beneath the table and up the stairs, toward the lantern gallery. At the first landing, she paused to look through a small leaded window to gain a better sense of the threat below, which is when she spied Cumberland at the lighthouse door. Angèle was shocked: Cumberland had perished in the fall, of that much she was certain. And the wendigo was mimicking his voice to bait her back into the woods, just as it had used Patrick's voice earlier.

"Angèle," the snake hissed in the potent voice of Marie Laveau.

"Mama!" Angèle exclaimed with relief. She was overjoyed that she was no longer alone in this unnerving fight and nearly broke down in tears.

The moment, however, did not last long. Cumberland was beating on the door: "Angèle!" he cried out one final time.

"The boy is cursed," said the snake. "Do not go back!"

"Can he be saved?" Angèle asked.

"As long as he has not yet consumed human flesh, then the death of the wendigo that infected him should set the boy free," she said. "But, you'll need silver."

"I'll never get close enough to use it without myself being infected—or worse. I'm going to burn it," Angèle said.

The snake gave no sign of Marie's approval.

Angèle continued climbing the stairs, now three at a time. She passed by the children's room on her way to the keeper's bedchamber. She hadn't any children of her own, but all of her friends had been taken from her. She couldn't even imagine the existential pain Aoife suffered while immured within those walls. How often did the violent scene of Caleb wrestling them from her clutches and tearing into them with his new fangs play over in her mind? How often did she blame herself for not doing more to save them? Or was it the death of Grainne—no one's fault but her own—that haunted her eternally? What, Angèle wondered, while looking at those three small, empty beds, would trouble her in death.

She didn't have long to ponder her regrets, so she flew up the stairs and into the keeper's bedchamber. When she arrived, she set Damballa on the floor near the bed and climbed the mountain of furniture through the hatch.

"Lock it behind you," the snake instructed.

"What about, Damballa," Angèle worried.

"She will be fine," her mother's voice assured her. Then,

before the hatch slammed shut, she said, "Angèle, *Ibos pend cor a yo.*"

"I understand," Angèle said, then closed the hatch and spun the locking wheel.

Three stories below, Caleb, the ancient wendigo, grasped the metal entryway door in his massive talons and crumpled it like a piece of tinfoil as he peeled it clean off the hinges. He had grown too tall to crouch through the modest opening, so Cumberland strode through the rupture and up the stairs. He could smell Angèle's fear wafting down from above. It had the reek of spoiled meat and ammonia that made him salivate. When he arrived in the bedchamber, Angèle was nowhere to be found, but his craving proved impossible to exorcise. He moved clumsily toward the hatch that he knew would take him into the watch room where Angèle would be trapped.

Just as Cumberland raised his foot to climb toward the piled furniture, Damballa struck from beneath the bed, so fast that even the young wendigo did not have time to react, despite its new supernatural speed. In seconds, the snake had coiled herself around Cumberland's torso and began constricting. With each breath he took, Damballa squeezed tighter, exerting perilous pressure to stop Cumberland's circulatory function and induce cardiac arrest. But the tighter she coiled, the harder and faster his heart pumped.

Cumberland convulsed in rage. He grasped the snake's midsection and pulled, unfurling it from his body with ease. Confused, Damballa struck repeatedly at his face with her dozens of recurved, needle-like teeth, to no avail. Though bleeding tremendously from the lacerations, Cumberland placed his other hand on the snake and tore her tenacious body in half. He flung Damballa's dismembered corpse to the ground without a second thought and rushed to the locked hatch. He wrenched at it with all his might and ravenous fury but was repeatedly denied access to Angèle. Cumberland leapt from the bed, splashed through the warm pool of python blood, and stormed out of the bedchamber looking for any way to satiate his hunger. Once outside, Cumberland communicated his failure telepathically to Caleb who immediately summoned the midnight darkness to unleash an arctic cyclone.

The supernatural wind beat against the lighthouse and rattled the lantern gallery windows, threatening to shatter Angèle's protection from the elements at any moment. She worked as quickly as her shaking hands would allow, feeding a frayed length of manila rope into a barrel of paraffin oil amidst the crates of phosphorus. The other end she carried with her through the infested watch room and back into the relative safety of Aoife's bedchamber, where she found Damballa's bloody remains.

Angèle let the oil-soaked rope hang from the ceiling and jumped down from the bed to inspect the massacre. She knelt in Damballa's blood and prayed that her mother dispossessed the snake's body before it was too late. Angèle then bent further toward the floor and coated her hands in the thick syrup, which she smeared across her face. "*Se pa kriye ki leve lamò,*" she sang, reaching her hand into the snake's belly—between her liver and esophagus—to retrieve her heart. Angèle closed her hand gently around the heart and pulled it free. She placed it gingerly into a pocket hidden in the folds of her dress and waited.

Outside, the Stygian storm raged around the brittle lighthouse. Caleb took flight, walking effortlessly upon the wind to the lantern gallery above. Meanwhile, Cumberland stalked the base. Angèle heard Caleb land with a crash on the walkway above; his taloned feet screamed against the metal, sending chills down her spine. Another crash followed, and then the tickling of glass window shards against the oil jars: a sweet song announcing Caleb's homecoming. Angèle's lips twisted into a crooked smile as she ignited the rope—a blue flame raced along the saturated fibers and into the makeshift combustion chamber filled with paraffin and phosphorus. The sneaking flame and the unsuspecting wendigo arrived inside the lantern gallery simultaneously. The red of Caleb's eyes faded to black as he watched, helpless, as the fire roared along the rope and disappeared into an oil barrel. The subsequent blast engulfed the indignant creature in a tangle of flames that instantly devoured its desiccated skin and reduced the wendigo's ancient bones to ash. The explosion that followed scattered Caleb's charred remains across the Champlain Valley.

The blast demolished the upper-floors of the centuries-old lighthouse, leaving Angèle exposed beneath the stars. The storm had died with the wendigo, revealing a crisp winter sky alight with celestial glister. Angèle was miraculously unharmed but shaken. It took her a moment to gather her wits, but as soon as she had, Angèle rushed down the stairs and into the night. She hoped to find Cumberland released from his psychosis. There was no immediate sign of him in the clearing, so she followed the tracks he had made in the snow, circumnavigating the lighthouse. Near the cellar doors, she found a mess of prints, indicating that Cumberland had tried to access the storeroom below. Whether he was unable to do so, or if Caleb's death had released Cumberland from the wendigo curse before he could pry open the doors, Angèle couldn't be sure. In any event, it appeared that Cumberland had wandered off into the woods. For where Angèle's single set of distressed tracks exited the trees another, larger footprint showed Cumberland's avenue of retreat.

Angèle contemplated going after him. He must be confused and scared, she reasoned. She was mostly afraid that Cumberland would remember what had happened to him—and the things he had done—while infected by the wendigo's curse. The psychological scarring would be tremendous, perhaps fatal. That settled it, Angèle would have to brave the woods to make sure that Cumberland didn't end his own life—either out of regret or the malevolent influence of the pukwudgie. She knew of a few healers in New Orleans who might be able to persuade him to forget the ordeal or at least help him to rationalize the madness. Then, just as Angèle was about to enter the woods, the pukwudgie appeared before her.

"Kyre," it hissed furiously. "Kyre, kyre." The creature waddled violently from among the trees and motioned irritably with its paw for Angèle to approach.

Her thoughts about Cumberland darkened with the presence of the pukwudgie. She knew that if he had returned to his natural state, it would not take the faeries long to prompt his death—if he survived the transformation at all. Without the wendigo's supernatural shell to protect his famished and broken body, Cumberland might be dead already.

"Kyre," the pukwudgie continued coaxing Angèle closer to the trees. She hadn't moved, but its invitation was unrelenting. Then, in no uncertain terms, she heard it say, "We want you, here." A field of luminous eyes exploded into view across the darkness behind the lone faery at the edge of the woods. Looming in the distance, behind the hoard of pukwudgie, as if commanding a devoted army, trembled the insidious embers of two seething, wendigo eyes. Angèle could not make out Cumberland's form against the black of the night, but his gaze carried accusation within it. He had feasted; whether upon Patrick, Absalom, or Thomas, Angèle could not know. But he had consummated the curse.

Angèle had nowhere to hide now that the lighthouse had been breached. And if the wendigo could penetrate the lighthouse, it might, too, be able to stalk from the cursed woods to hunt in cities and towns. In spite of misfortune and disappointment, Angèle's intrepid spirit had not wavered. She repeated aloud her mother's farewell evocation of the melancholy Igbo: "*Ibos pend cor a yo.*" Like Aoife before her, Angèle would sacrifice herself to confine the beast within the Cloven Rock wilderness. And she hadn't a moment more to spare.

Angèle hurried into the lighthouse through the open entryway and retrieved her pack of rum grenades. She then pulled two of the dining chairs into the doorway and set the canvas bag on top of them before lighting it on fire. Even before the bag exploded, Angèle had begun heaping the remaining chairs and a few of the roll-top desk drawers into the doorway to feed the fire. When the improvised grenades detonated, the flames created a barrier that the wendigo dared not cross. Angèle pushed the desk and the Turk's wooden trunk into the fire. Surveying her work, and pleased with the burn, she turned her attention to the blackened hearth across the room.

With a slight stick of white chalk in her left hand, Angèle drew a skull and crossbones at the back of the firebox and placed upon the grate a prayer card painted with the image of St. Martin de Porres. She sprinkled the picture with *sal negra* and lit it on fire, completing her makeshift *manjè mò* altar. Angèle then shattered the neck of her last remaining rum bottle against the plinth. Shards of glass fell into the liquid, but Angèle paid it no heed. She pulled Damballa's heart from her pocket and submerged it in the rum, which instantly turned the color of molten barley sugar. This, too, she lit ablaze and called out to the fearsome guédé of malice, Baron Kriminel. "First Murderer! Master of the veils! I invoke you to pronounce swift judgment upon the life of Angèle Paris D'Arcantel."

Angèle drew forth a small knife from her belt and dragged it along her arm. She cried out in pain to appease the Baron, and allowed her blood to flow into the fiery rum. "Cain of the Carribean, condemn me to death!" Angèle submerged her hand into the fire and drew forth Damballa's blackened heart from the rum. She held the now beating heart before the memento mori that she had chalked upon the firebox as an offering to Baron Kriminel, then bit through the char into its supple tissue and tore a piece free. "Eat with me this last supper."

From behind Angèle, the Baron's skeletal hand reached out and took Damballa's heart from her hand. Angèle's eyes followed the cuff of his tattered shirt, festooned with black rooster feathers, to his obscured face, upon which he wore a human skull like a helmet. He dressed in the clothes of a colonial planter: light trousers, a black coat and a dark red cravat. Around his waist hung a belt of shrunken heads, and he carried with him a sack that Angèle knew to be filled with the souls he had collected. Baron Kriminel opened his mouth and placed Damballa's entire heart inside. Without chewing even once, he swallowed it whole into the void of his gullet. Angèle was sick with fear before this harrowing presence. She handed him the broken bottle of spiced rum, which he drank to the dreg. When he had finished, the Baron gnawed the glass with masochistic pleasure.

"Please, make it quick," Angèle requested. "We don't have much time."

"Your wendigo would not dare confront me, Angèle Paris D'Arcantel. We have all the time that I require," the Baron boasted, brandishing a gilded fork and spoon. Without warning, he drove the fork into the base of Angèle's neck and twisted it thrice round. Angèle's spinal cord twirled upon the Baron's fork as if a limp noodle. Baron Kriminel yanked his fork free and ate with relish her saccharine nervous tissue.

Freed from her physical body, Angèle's spirit watched with disgust as the Baron feasted on her remains. "Nothing to fear now, my dear," the Baron assured her. "Except, perhaps, an eternity of isolation." He clucked. "But alas, I am a busy lwa and must be on my way." When he had reached his fill, the Baron wiped his lips on a silken handkerchief. He used the silver toe of his black boot to push Angèle's body into the flames. Her hair caught first and sent a flare up the chimney. The fire crawled along her back, scorching her clothes. Smoke infused with the essence of *sal negra* leeched to her crisping skin.

"More payments to claim?" Angèle said sardonically.

"Indeed. Your world is a terrible place," said Baron Kriminel. And then he was gone.

Angèle stood alone in the ruins of the Cloven Rock lighthouse, watching her body smolder on the fire as the embers in the entry way cooled.

Once the fire had completely extinguished, Cumberland entered the lighthouse. He was careful to avoid stepping on the plate of silver that had formed over the threshold, where Angèle's chest of coins had melted and then cooled. He searched frantically for Angèle's body, which he could smell cooking. When he came upon her mangled and charred corpse in the hearth, he hunched over it as would any rabid animal, and fed.

Just as the wendigo demon had once inhabited the foul Onondaga salt that Fr. Simon Le Moyne sent to Aoife, and which it used as a conduit to possess her husband, Caleb, so, too the *sal negra* Angèle used to prepare her *manjè mò* pyre, thereby seasoning her own flesh, would incarcerate Cumberland within the cursed wood, evermore.

# Epilogue

# Fèt Gede

"Pukwudgie," Fausta breathed in amazement.

Her grandmother nodded. "We are safe here. It cannot leave the woods. Angèle sees to that."

"Angèle is...real?" Fausta asked in disbelief.

"Of course, child," said her grandmother. "I would not be false with you."

"But, why did you bring me here?" Fausta asked. "Who is Angèle to you?"

"No one," said the old woman, "but Lala Hopkins—the daughter of Hany Blackman and Cumberland Hopkins—was my great-great-grandmother."

Fausta looked down at the photograph that her grandmother had placed in her hands, "This isn't Angèle," she said, studying the woman's face that suddenly seemed to her more familiar.

"No," her grandmother confirmed. "That is Lala. We look similar, don't we?" She smiled, proud to bear the woman's resemblance.

"But, you said that a kelpie drowned and devoured Hany," Fausta objected. "How could she have survived to give birth?"

A harsh growl ripped from the pukwudgie's throat, startling Fausta.

Unflinching, her grandmother said, "You are looking through the glass, darkly. Like the púca, or the pukwudgie, kelpie are capable of both malevolence and beneficence."

"You mean that the kelpie who stole Hany Blackman away from Cumberland did so in order to rescue her?" Fausta asked.

"That is what I mean," her grandmother said.

"But, why?" Fausta challenged.

"Aoife's sacrifice," said her grandmother, simply. "The death of Aoife's unborn daughter, Grainne, assured the protection of every expecting mother that found herself within the cursed woods. The child Hany carried within her was not to be harmed. Not even Caleb could breach that contract."

"What happened to her, then? Hany?" Fausta said.

"Hany returned to New Orleans and entered into the care of Angèle's half-sister, Marie the Second, who later initiated Lala into vodou," her grandmother said.

"But, why did we make our Fèt Gede pilgrimage to these woods if our ancestors escaped and returned to New Orleans?" Fausta asked. "We could have just stayed home."

"We are here to ask lwa Zaka to rid our patriarch, Cumberland, of the wendigo curse," her grandmother said.

"Will that work?" Fausta asked.

A low rumble hummed along the two-lane highway that stretched far beyond the small town into the northern darkness. It was the first sound they had heard all evening other than the beckoning call of the pukwudgie. For a moment, Fausta thought it might be thunder creeping across the valley, but there wasn't a cloud in the sky above them. Soon, beaming headlights from a tanker truck poised to turn left into the 24-hour gas station lighted the vacant lot in which she and her grandmother stood.

"Look," Fausta said pointing to the pukwudgie. The creature's aggravated scowl had suspiciously transformed into an eager grin. It squealed a sinister laugh. "What do you suppose it's up to?" she asked her grandmother, who had turned to watch the lone traffic light change from fire-engine red to Kelly green. The tanker turned and lurched into the gas station. Its headlights stretched the women's shadows beyond the rusted train tracks and into the trees. Before her grandmother could even gasp, the puckwudgie shot forth a hairy claw and snatched Fausta by her shadow. Just as quickly, its other hand seized the woman by her own slender shadow, and dragged them both into the darkened depths of the forest, unnoticed.

# Endnotes

1   Posting: "Advice to Irish Emigrants," *Jeanie Johnston Tall Ships and Famine Museum*. Custom House Quay, Dublin, Ireland.

2   Mary Wilkinson, "Partial Passenger List for the Ship Agnes," *The Ships List*. October 30, 2006. Accessed November 1, 2017. URL: http://www.theshipslist.com/ships/passengerlists/agn es1847.shtml

3   W.B. Yeats, "The Stolen Child," *The Stolen Child* (1889), *The Collected Works of W.B. Yeats: Volume I, The Poems*. Ed. Richard J. Finneran. Scribner, 1997. P. 16.

4   Simon Le Moyne, "Among the Salt Makers," excerpted from Le Moyne's private diary. *The Syracuse Standard*. 19 January 1878.

5   Northrop, "Slave Dealing in New Orleans—An Auction," *New York Daily Tribune*. 26 January, 1848. Ann Arbor District Library, Ann Arbor, MI. Accessed November 1, 2017. http://signalofliberty.aadl.org/signalofliberty/SL_18460420-p1-03

6   *New Orleans Bee*. 11 April 1834. Jefferson Parish Library, New Orleans, LA. Accessed November 1, 2017. URL: http://nobee.jefferson.lib.la.us/Vol-009/04_1834/1834_04_0034.pdf

7   "Come, come, whoever you are. Wanderer, worshiper, lover of leaving. It doesn't matter. Ours is not a caravan of despair. Come, even if you have broken your vows a thousand times. Come, yet again, come, come." — Jalaluddin Rumi.

8   William Collins (1721–1759), "Ode on the Popular Superstitions of the Highlands of Scotland."

9   Charles Dickens, *American Notes for General Circulation*, 1842.

**Recent bestsellers from Cosmic Egg Books are:**

## The Zombie Rule Book
A Zombie Apocalypse Survival Guide
Tony Newton
The book the living-dead don't want you to have!
Paperback: 978-1-78279-334-2 ebook: 978-1-78279-333-5

## Cryptogram
Because the Past is Never Past
Michael Tobert
Welcome to the dystopian world of 2050, where three lovers are
haunted by echoes from eight-hundred years ago.
Paperback: 978-1-78279-681-7 ebook: 978-1-78279-680-0

## Purefinder
Ben Gwalchmai
London, 1858. A child is dead; a man is blamed and dragged
through hell in this Dantean tale of loss, mystery and fraternity.
Paperback: 978-1-78279-098-3 ebook: 978-1-78279-097-6

## 600ppm
A Novel of Climate Change
Clarke W. Owens
Nature is collapsing. The government doesn't want you to know
why. Welcome to 2051 and 600ppm.
Paperback: 978-1-78279-992-4 ebook: 978-1-78279-993-1

## Creations
William Mitchell
Earth 2040 is on the brink of disaster. Can Max Lowrie stop the
self-replicating machines before it's too late?
Paperback: 978-1-78279-186-7 ebook: 978-1-78279-161-4

**The Gawain Legacy**
Jon Mackley
If you try to control every secret, secrets may end up controlling
you.
Paperback: 978-1-78279-485-1 ebook: 978-1-78279-484-4


Readers of ebooks can buy or view any of these bestsellers by
clicking on the live link in the title. Most titles are published
in paperback and as an ebook. Paperbacks are available in
traditional bookshops. Both print and ebook formats are
available online.
Find more titles and sign up to our readers' newsletter at
http://www.johnhuntpublishing.com/fiction
Follow us on Facebook at https://www.facebook.com/JHPfiction
and Twitter at https://twitter.com/JHPFiction